SOMEDAY REMEMBER

J.C. MacDonald

Someday Remember

It was early autumn in 1983 and Billy Maguire sat at the dining table in his parent's house, tucking into some toast and marmalade with a cup of steaming hot tea. He had returned from London late the night before and, preferring not to wake his mum Pauline by rummaging around the kitchen looking for a snack, he had gone to bed hungry. But now here he was, feeling right at home in this familiar environment. He felt a sense of warmth and comfort as he looked around his parents' home despite the complex situation he found himself in. His gaze wandered as he ate, his eyes drifted to the antique upright piano his Uncle James had passed down to him when it had become clear that Billy had inherited the family passion for making music. He felt an overpowering urge to take a seat on the vintage stool and create something beautiful. This instrument always inspired him; he used it as a starting point for many of his songs.

The piano sat in front of a midnight blue wall that was decorated with wood chip wallpaper, the surface partially hidden by an oversized elephant print. To his right was a wooden panelled wall that curved gracefully around the edges and was completely covered by a gigantic map of the world in which each country had been assigned its own unique colour.

An imposing picture of Alastair, Billy's father, sat in one of two framed photographs propped up on top of the piano, it struck Billy as strange that there weren't any images of his parents together, he'd only seen individual ones, discounting the wedding album of course. Alastair was an old-fashioned, candid Glaswegian hailing from Clydebank to the west of the city. He had a thick head of white hair and a knowing, seen it all face but no other defining features. In the past, he had been a popular big band leader and saxophonist, however, when Anna, his first child was born, he had chosen to take another path in order to be able to spend more time with his family. His wit was razor sharp, sometimes veering into arrogance, but he was an honest and hardworking man who now earned a living as a self-employed stock taker.

Delicately placed on the other side of the piano sat Pauline's photo in its silver frame. Billy observed her with admiration; he thought she was beautiful despite being in her early fifties, her delicate skin as smooth as porcelain and eyes brown like chestnuts. He had never seen his mum without her hair perfectly in place, her subtle makeup delicately applied and she always looked immaculate, regardless of what she wore.

He turned his head and glanced behind him. Against the wall sat an old mahogany sideboard that matched the table he was sitting at. Covering the surface were ornaments, trinkets and various assortments of souvenirs that had been brought back from India by Billy's grandad Stephen when he'd been stationed overseas. Hand carved ivory and brass candlesticks, and a highly polished silver teapot sat amongst numerous other items but Billy had never understood why anyone would want such things on display. He looked back to see his mum standing in the doorway.

Pauline's face contorted with a mix of rage and sadness as she spat out her words. "You were the sweetest child, until you reached 16! That's when it all changed. It was like you had been replaced by some other entity, the second Danny Dipstick there got his hands on you!" Her gaze shot daggers towards Billy's crotch and her voice dropped to a low growl. "God knows how your dad and I ever produced you and your sister!"

Billy's older sister Anna was a smart and defiant free spirit. Her wild Henna red hair gave her an alluring beauty that had attracted many admirers in the local area. On more than one occasion, Alastair had to escort a broken-hearted figure away from the doorstep after she'd dismissed them earlier in the evening and they'd been unable to accept it. She'd left home to go travelling with her best friend Sheila about four years ago and she was currently living on a kibbutz in Israel with a soldier called Saul, they would be returning to meet the family soon, a meeting his father was desperately trying to push out of his mind.

Billy felt a knot form in his stomach as his mother's words hit him like a ton of bricks. He had expected some kind of lecture, but nothing like this. The pain in her eyes made him realise that she wasn't just angry, she was hurt. He wanted to say something to make it better, but the words wouldn't come. Instead, he looked down at his plate and pushed his toast around.

Pauline took a deep breath and composed herself before continuing. "I know you think you're a man now, but you're still my son. And I won't stand by and watch you destroy yourself."

Billy flinched, anger and hurt bubbling up inside him. But he didn't want to argue with her. Instead, he took a deep breath and tried to calm himself down. "I'm sorry, Mum," he said, his voice steady. "I know I've made some mistakes, but I'm trying to make things right." As if sensing his thoughts, Pauline spoke again. "I love you, Billy," she said, stepping closer to him and putting a hand on his shoulder. "No matter what, you'll always be my son."

Billy felt a lump form in his throat. Despite everything, he knew that she loved him, and he loved her too. He reached up and covered her hand with his own. "I've no idea what to do Mum, I think I want to be involved but I don't know what I can offer. The last time I rang, Dennis answered, he told me exactly what he thought of me then said that Jessica doesn't want to see me and not to ring this number again."

Jessica Matthews, or 'Jess' as Billy called her, had been his ex girlfriend. They'd met after a show Billy's band had been playing in a village near Nottingham, where Jess was attending university. They'd made plans to meet up the following weekend in London, but it had been nothing more than a fling, they'd only seen each other five or six times. Now here he was, waiting for news of the birth of his first child!

"I know love" began Pauline, "I've been in touch with Marion," Jess' mother who was known for her compassion and understanding. "We've been trying to find a way through this mess. Dennis," who was Jess' father, a man of few words and even fewer emotions, "has made it quite clear he doesn't want anything to do with you, but Marion is willing to talk. She said she'll keep us posted on the baby's arrival and maybe we can go and visit once things have calmed down a bit." Billy felt a glimmer of hope at his mother's words. Maybe there was a chance for him to be a part of his child's life after all. He just needed to figure out how to make things right with Jess and her family. "Thanks, Mum," he said gratefully. "I don't know what I'd do without you." Pauline smiled warmly at her son and squeezed his shoulder before turning to leave the room.

Billy moved towards the piano. He knew that he was different from most people, but he didn't see anything wrong with that. He just wished that his family could accept him for who he was, instead of trying to change him. He was a musician first and foremost, or so he told himself, he was going to be successful! He hadn't planned on having a child in his life. How would it fit in? He understood he'd have to be part of its life and contribute financially and emotionally but how was he going to do that? He was struggling to look after himself!

As he sat down at the piano and ran his fingers over the keys, Billy felt his mind drift away from the present and into a world of music, where everything made sense. He began to play a soft melody, letting the notes fill the room with a sense of calm. Music had always been his escape, his sanctuary, and he knew that it was the one thing that could never be taken away from him.

He closed his eyes and let the music guide him, trying to find some peace in the chaos of his life. As he played, he could feel his mother's presence behind him. She was listening, and he hoped that the music would bring her some comfort.

As he played, he began to realise that he had been running away from his problems for too long. He needed to face them head-on if he wanted to move forward with his life.

The melody changed, becoming more hopeful and uplifting. Billy's fingers danced over the keys, the notes ringing out through the house. He felt a sense of clarity wash over him. He knew what he needed to do.

He stood up from the piano, turning to face his mother. "I need to go and see Jess," he said, his voice filled with determination. "I need to make things right. I need to be a part of my child's life."

Pauline looked at him with a mixture of worry and pride. "I'll support you no matter what," she said, her voice soft. "Just promise me that you'll be careful."

"Don't worry, mum," smiled Billy before the ringing of a telephone in the hallway shifted the atmosphere once more.

CHAPTER TWO

Pauline returned to the dining room and fell heavily into her chair. Her face was ashen, pain etched into her features. She began to cry, tears streaming down her cheeks as she murmured,

"She's gone, Billy. Jess gave birth to a little girl, but there were complications. The baby was breech, and the umbilical cord had wrapped itself around her neck during the birth. She didn't make it."

As Billy processed the news, a wave of despair came crashing over him. He'd been waiting for months for this day, but now what? There had been times lately when he'd seriously considered being a father, but deep down he'd been petrified about it all.

The realisation of his own recklessness hit him hard, how could he have been a father if he couldn't even take control of his own life? He was constantly running away from reality, wasting his time with women, alcohol and drugs, music was his only true passion.

As his mum continued to cry, Billy sat there motionless; the news had taken his breath away. He didn't know what to say or how to react. All he could think of was the sound of his own heartbeat, pounding in his chest. He felt feelings inside him that he couldn't describe.

He had never been good with comforting people, especially when he himself was struggling to cope. But he knew that he had to try. He stood up and walked over to his mother, pulling her into a hug.

Pauline sobbed into his chest, and Billy felt a pang of guilt. He had been so selfish, so focused on his own problems that he had never truly thought what this might be doing to her.

He held her for a long time, until her tears subsided and her breathing evened out. Then he pulled away and looked into her eyes. The guilt was evident in his voice as he spoke. "Mum, I'm so sorry. I've been so focused on myself that I haven't thought about how this situation could affect you. I don't know what to do and I'm here again asking for your help with yet another problem."

Pauline nodded sadly, tears still streaming down her face. She stroked his arm gently and said, "We'll get through this together."

Billy smiled weakly in response and the two of them sat there in silence for what felt like hours, trying to process the enormity of what had just happened.

Pauline was the first to speak. "It's done now," she stated firmly, "except for Jessica's family, nobody knows anything about this. So I think we should keep it that way. I had no idea how I was going to tell your dad, but thank god I won't have to do so now. You must promise me, Billy, you won't say a thing to anyone about any of this. We both know that you can't take care of yourself let alone a child, so although this is an awful situation and I feel terrible for that family's suffering, we should try to make the best of it. Your dad still hasn't got over Mary yet, if he found out about this too, his heart would be broken all over again."

Mary had been Billy's younger sister. She was two years younger than him but she had only lived for a couple weeks due to a brain defect, which had made her survival impossible. He'd had a faint memory of another baby at some point, but he couldn't exactly recall who it was.

Billy nodded, his guilt only growing. He couldn't imagine what it was like for his mother to lose her own daughter and now this.

He had always been distant from his family, but in that moment, he realised that he needed them more than ever. "I promise, Mum. I won't say a word," he said softly, the weight of the promise heavy on his shoulders.

"I'm going to change, Mum," he said suddenly. Pauline turned to look at him, surprised. "What do you mean, Billy?"

"I mean, I'm going to stop running away from my problems. I'm going to get my life together. For you, for Dad, for Mary, and for that little girl who never got to live. I want to make something of myself, and I want to help people. I want to be a better person."

Pauline smiled sadly, "That's a lovely thought Billy but we both know it's just another empty promise. One of many you've made. Stay for the rest of the weekend and say hello to your dad when he gets back, then get yourself home to London and throw yourself into your life there. There's nothing you can do about what's happened, I think it's best that you know that Dennis was never going to allow you to have anything to do with the baby! You wouldn't have been able to see her. All I want from you now is to promise me you'll learn something from all this and be a little more responsible in future."

Billy was crestfallen, his mother's words like a dagger through his soul. He knew that his mother was right. He had made empty promises before, and he had never followed through with them.

He nodded slowly, "I promise, Mum. I'll do better. I'll make you proud."

Pauline smiled softly, "I'm already proud of you, Billy. You're a good lad, a little reckless maybe and never slow to press that self-destruct button but you have a kind soul and caring heart. I just wish you'd think more carefully about the repercussions of some of your actions. Remember, I won't always be here to clean up after you."

Billy sat in silence for a moment, staring at his hands. The thought of going back to his life in London filled him with dread. He had never felt so lost and alone.

He stood up and walked to the window, staring out at the rain-soaked streets. "Ok, I'll stay for the weekend," he said finally. "But after that, I need to figure out what I'm going to do with my life."

Pauline patted his shoulder, "Why don't you go out for a walk or something? Clear your head a little."

"Yeah why not" said Billy; maybe some fresh air and time alone would help.

Billy walked through the rain-soaked streets, his hands buried deep in his pockets. The rain had always brought him comfort; he found the sound of it soothing and the smell of the damp ground comforting.

He thought back to his life in London, the endless parties, the meaningless one nighters, the constant haze of drugs and alcohol.

He trudged out onto the muddy towpath, rain dripping off his jacket and onto the puddled ground. He glanced into the murky canal water, a thin sheen of oil coating its surface in rainbow swirls. The surrounding reeds clung to the sides of the canal, weighed down by a multitude of plastic bottles and cans; he wondered why no one seemed to care about where their discarded rubbish ended up.

At a nearby lock, he watched as a young woman fiddled with the gate mechanism while an older, scruffy-looking man with an unkempt beard and greasy hair expertly steered the long, brightly coloured barge into place.

Billy knelt on the banks of the canal, his gaze drawn to the old railway sheds across the water. He watched as two small figures explored the forgotten land, just like he and his friends had done years ago. In his mind's eye he could still see the bustling atmosphere that these grounds used to exude, freight trains loading up with goods, managers shouting orders and workers going about their daily duties. Now the tracks were covered in weeds, twisted metal poles propping up derelict buildings, and distant memories of its former glory whispered through the air.

He trudged along, his mind exploding in thought until he eventually came to a stop outside the house that had brought him so much joy in the past. He decided there and then to leave the earlier events behind him and focus on everything else life had to offer. He would keep his word to his mother and never bring up the subject of his child ever again.

Chapter Three

Billy found himself in the tiny room that had been his ever since his family moved into their own home. Anna, being the eldest and a bossy little madam, had taken it upon herself to choose the best bedroom for herself.

He glanced around taking in the details. A single bed was tucked into one corner, its sheets and pillowcase boasting a bright mix of blue, pink, and white stripes. A lime green blanket weighted down by an emerald green eiderdown. In the opposite corner, an old wardrobe had been built in to save space and along the other wall was a long mahogany cupboard that had had enough storage room for his clothes and toys when he was younger.

Now his mother had somehow managed to squeeze in a small table with a chair towards the centre of the room. An antique Singer sewing machine sat on top of it, needles and reels of thread scattered across its surface.

The room seemed cramped and lacked space but it was warm and cosy, all Billy needed at the moment.

He stepped out onto the landing and admired himself in the full-length mirror that was fixed to the far wall. Amid the whirlwind of events that had already claimed the whole day, he found time to slow down and critically examine himself. He fell somewhere in between average and good-looking, depending on how much effort he put into his appearance. He had a strong jawline and bright blue eyes that were accentuated by the height of his cheekbones. He'd inherited his mother's clear skin that had left him free of acne and unsightly blemishes which gave him more confidence than he would have had otherwise, he hadn't hit every branch on his way down the ugly tree but he'd definitely glanced off a couple. His hair was cut in a shoulder length spiked mullet that he had bleached white. He wore his favourite bands T-shirt that had a large middle finger on the chest peeking out of an expensive black leather jacket with long fringes around his arms and down across the back, they flowed down into his faded blue jeans with fraying at the knees and thigh, tucked into his favourite black and cream snakeskin cowboy boots. His signature black eyeliner completed what he thought was a stylish look.

Anna's black and white cat, Thomas, who she'd brought home from the riding stables about ten years ago was asleep in front of his sister's bedroom door. Some might say he was there to protect her room until her return, while others would argue he just liked the morning sunshine that beamed through the landing window and made that spot warm. Billy received an unimpressed gaze when he walked by, Thomas slowly getting up, stretching, and then reclining again with his back to him.

He marched down the stairs and into the living room, prompting Pauline to ask in surprise if he was going somewhere.

"Yes," Billy replied cautiously. "Why?"

"I don't think it's a good idea, given everything that's happened," she said.

He defended his decision to leave, saying he was going mad staying at home and wanted to see if anyone else was around.

"But do you think the eyeliner is too much?" Pauline asked. "You're not in London you know, not everyone around here understands this style. Remember how you got into trouble when you went out during your last visit?"

He remembered all too well. He had gone out with some old friends and he'd been confronted by a jealous ex boyfriend of a girl he'd seen the night before. Rather than see sense and apologise, thus keeping the situation calm, Billy had chosen to let the alcohol speak for him, "you should be thanking me mate," he'd told him "I did you a favour, she's a right fucking slag, I'm amazed I managed to keep it up!" The resulting punch to the mouth had dislodged two of his front teeth, cutting short the evening and resulting in an expensive dental bill to repair the damage.

"I'll be fine mum, I promise. I won't be too late." he said, Pauline wasn't so sure.

He walked out of the house, the cold autumn air hitting him like a slap in the face. His breath steamed in the air as he walked down the quiet street, the only sound being his boots clicking against the pavement. He pulled his collar up, trying to fend off the chill, and made his way to the local pub.

He pushed open the door to the pub, and the warm, smoky air hit him. He looked around, seeing a few regulars huddled around the bar, nursing pints of beer. He nodded at them, made his way to the bar and ordered a pint. He walked to a booth that was empty, the red leather seat cracked and worn from years of use. He slid in, feeling the familiar creak of the seat beneath him.

He settled back in the booth, taking in the familiar sights and smells of the pub. He lit a cigarette and watched as the regulars chatted and joked, their laughter ringing out in the cosy space.

As he sat there, sipping his pint and smoking his cigarette, Billy couldn't help but feel a sense of relief. It was good to be out of the house, here, he could be himself.

He finished his cigarette and ordered another pint, feeling a warmth spreading through his body as the alcohol took effect. He watched as a group of girls walked in, their giggles and whispers filling the air. Billy felt a pang of longing, wishing he had someone to share his life with.

But as he watched the girls, he realised that he didn't want just anyone. He wanted someone special who would accept him for who he was. He wanted someone to love and someone who would love him.

He finished his pint and stood up, feeling a sudden surge of energy. He walked over to the jukebox, looking through the selection of songs. He punched in a few numbers and smiled as the opening chords of his favourite song filled the pub.

He made his way back to the booth, tapping his feet and mouthing the words to the song. People looked at him curiously, but Billy didn't care. He was in his element, and nothing could bring him down.

As the song ended, he downed another beer and stood up, feeling a bit unsteady on his feet. He stumbled a bit, but managed to make his way out of the pub and onto the street.

He took in a deep breath of the cool air and started walking, feeling a sense of freedom.

As he walked the deserted streets, he felt his heart pounding in his chest with excitement. The alcohol had made him feel invincible, and he was ready to take on the world. He made a plan to return to London and leave all memories of the weekend behind. He would focus on his music, believing that love would come his way soon enough. Until then, he decided to concentrate on himself. He called in at the off licence on the corner and bought himself a half bottle of vodka then made his way back to his parents house.

He unlocked the door, slipped inside and closed it quietly behind him. He felt like he was sneaking up on life as he stood in the darkness and poured himself a generous glass of vodka. He took off his boots so he wouldn't wake anyone and put an album on the music centre in the corner of the living room. As soon as he put on the headphones and turned up the volume, he was lost in the music and forgot about everything except for that moment.

Chapter Four

Billy stirred in a haze of confusion, a steady thumping echoing between his ears. He had no idea what time it was or any recollection of the previous night's events.

He could hear voices downstairs but couldn't make out what they were saying. He stumbled out of bed, dressed himself in last night's clothes and made his way downstairs.

"Hello son," beamed his father in a thick Scottish accent, "you hit the big time yet?"

Billy winced, his head pounding. "No not yet, just thought I'd come home for a quiet weekend and see my wonderful parents," he said with a hint of sarcasm.

"No, I didn't think so," said Alastair, the smile fading "you're not going to with that bunch of jokers either, I've told you before to get out on your own. You're a good songwriter and you play guitar well but there's a million just like you. If you think dressing up like a big Jessie with makeup all over your face is the way forward forget it. You'll need something else. Get yourself in a working band and earn a living, dreaming about the big time won't get you anywhere unless you put in the hard work!"

Billy had grown accustomed to his father's straightforward attitude, harsh though it sometimes was, his dad was a fair and truthful man, and more often than not, Billy would reluctantly agree with him. He remembered after one particularly unsuccessful game of football when he was younger, his dad had praised some areas where Billy had shined, but then let him know that "you'll never make it as a footballer as long as you've got a hole in your arse!"

While Billy knew deep down that he wasn't quite good enough to make it, he thought there might have been kinder ways to put it. Despite this, his father's blunt approach had made him more resilient to criticism.

"What do you know about the music business Dad?" countered Billy.

"More than you do son. I was in it for years, don't forget, I've forgotten more than you'll ever know."

"Oh yes I forgot you're a musician yourself," said Billy, "you're so perfect and talented."

"Hardly!" retorted his father, "but I'm realistic! You've got to get out there and play."

Billy could feel the anger rising. "You're so full of

shit!" he said, "you're not going to tell me what I should be doing."

"Isn't that what you want?" said Alastair, puzzled. "To get out there and play, get yourself noticed, start earning a living. We've given you every opportunity and it's up to you. If you want to be a rock star, get out there."

"That's not how it works anymore," said Billy defensively, "it's all about contacts and connections now."

"Bollocks," said Alastair, "you're never going to get anywhere with that attitude. If you're out there playing and you're any good, the contacts and connections will find you."

At that moment Pauline put her head around the door. "You two have only been in the same room for five minutes and you're arguing already, why can't we just have one pleasant weekend without you two bickering all the time?"

"I'm sorry mum," said Billy sadly and he sat down on the sofa.

Alastair's words cut deep and Billy knew he spoke from experience. He had been a successful musician until he'd decided to give it up and spend more time with his new daughter, Billy didn't dare tell his father but knew he was right. He knew he was a good musician himself but he wasn't that good.

He had never thought about his job prospects, the thought that he might not make it to the big time having never really crossed his mind. He had always believed that he was a cut above most of the others, that he would be one of those special few who made it. But now the doubts were creeping in, the songwriter in him knew that he was good but not great. His playing could carry him only so far but he just didn't have the confidence to leave the band and try on his own.

"Can I go upstairs for a shower?" he asked, getting up and hoping to slip away without angering his parents any further. "I need to get back to London today."

"Go ahead, love," Pauline smiled. "Come down when you're finished and we can have a drink before dinner. Maybe you and your dad can talk about something you both agree on."

He made his way upstairs, feeling defeated. He knew his father was right, but he didn't want to admit it. As he stepped into the shower, he let the hot water wash over him, trying to wash away his doubts and fears. But they clung to him like a bad smell, refusing to budge.

He couldn't help but think about his band mates, the ones he had left behind in London. He loved them all, but they were struggling just like he was. Maybe his father was right, maybe he needed to find a way to earn a living and make a name for himself.

But as the hot water continued to beat down on him, Billy's mind began to wander. He thought about the late nights in dingy pubs, the rush of adrenaline when the crowd cheered, the feeling of being on top of the world when they played a perfect set. That was what he lived for, that was what he wanted.

He knew he couldn't give up on his dream, not yet. He had to find a way to make it work, to be the one in a million that his father had talked about. He had to keep writing, keep playing, keep pushing himself to be better. He couldn't let his doubts hold him back.

As he stepped out of the shower and dried himself off, Billy felt a new determination take hold of him. He would find a way to make it work, no matter what it took. He would prove his father wrong, and he would do it his way.

With a new sense of purpose, he made his way back downstairs to join his parents for a drink.

He sat on the sofa, idly leafing through the Sunday papers, still not used to the quiet of a house without his band mates and their endless daily banter. They were still young and in their early twenties, but the music scene in London was full of bands just like them, kids burning with the ambition to make it to the top. It had grown so much from when Billy's father had been a professional musician, change was the only constant.

Like so many others, Billy had fallen in love with music as a kid, and it had become his life. In his teens he had joined a succession of bands, the line up regularly changing as the other members struggled to find the commitment and determination that Billy displayed.

And his persistence had paid off, he had joined The

Innocent and they had started to gain a name for themselves. He had left his job as a screen printer in a factory and moved into the squalor of a shared house with the band living on beans on toast and cheap lager, but happy to be 'making it'. He smiled at the memory.

"You'll need to take the bus to the station," his dad spoke, cutting through his daydream. "Your mum and I are in no state to drive you after the drinks we've had. Look, I understand that I can be a bit tough on you sometimes but it is only because I have high hopes for you. You don't seem to realise that success requires hard work and luck. You seem to think that by somehow meeting the so-called 'right people', chasing every woman you can and dressing up is enough, but it won't get you very far. Find yourself one nice girl and have some self respect."

Billy prickled a little when his father spoke of getting one girl and respecting yourself, but he chose to stay silent. He recalled growing up in the big farmhouse where he was born, and how he'd sometimes have to go to his parents' bedroom for help and comfort after wetting the bed. One time, his dad had been alone in the room wearing only a dressing gown, telling him to go back to his own room. But then Billy had seen his mum at the back door saying goodbye to another couple while she herself wore nothing but a dressing gown, kissing them both on the lips as they parted. There were other similar occasions that Billy witnessed throughout childhood, but it wasn't until he was 13 when he'd found pictures in the sideboard of his mum and dad with an oriental looking woman, all of them in various states of undress, that the penny finally dropped. That's when he finally understood why his parents made regular trips on Saturdays and Wednesdays to what they called the "health club". It turned out that big band music wasn't the only kind of swinging they enjoyed!

Billy shook his head, trying to clear the memories from his mind as his mum called them to the table. They enjoyed a wonderful family dinner then Billy went upstairs to collect his things, gave his parents a quick hug, promising to come back soon, before making his way out to the bus stop.

Chapter Five

Billy looked out of the train window watching the countryside pass by in a blur. He felt a sense of restlessness in him, a need to move and keep moving. He wanted to get back and be with his band mates, to play music, forgetting about the devastating news he'd received over the weekend and the doubts that had plagued him earlier.

As he stepped off the train and made his way through the bustling station, he felt the apprehension build within him. He was back in the city he didn't particularly like, the city that had given him a chance to make something of himself admittedly but, it was a place that he didn't feel at home in. Nothing felt familiar and nothing felt comfortable.

He made his way through the busy streets, the sounds of the city ringing in his ears; the smell of street food and exhaust fumes filling his nostrils.

As he approached the door to the house he shared with the band a smile spread across his face. He couldn't wait to see his band mates, have some laughs, and play some music.

As he opened the door, his smile faded. The house was a mess, empty beer cans and pizza boxes strewn across the floor, the smell of stale smoke and unwashed clothes hanging in the air.

Paul, the bass player in the band, sprawled across the sofa, watching TV and barely registering his presence.

"Hey," he said, barely looking up. "How was your trip home?"

"It was fine," he replied, trying to keep the disappointment out of his voice. "How have things been here?"

Paul shrugged. "Same old, same old. We've got a gig next week, though. Should be good."

Billy nodded, feeling a touch of relief at the news. At least they had something to look forward to, something to focus on. He made his way to his room and dropped his bag on the bed. He had thought that coming back to the band would make everything better, but it seemed that his problems ran deeper than he had realised.

He made his way back to the living room, taking a seat next to Paul on the sofa. They watched TV in silence for a few minutes, before Billy finally spoke up.

"I've been thinking," he said, his voice quiet. "Maybe we need to change things up. Try something new."

Paul raised an eyebrow. "What do you mean?"

"I mean...maybe it's time to stop playing the same old bars and clubs. Maybe we need to try and get a record deal, get our music out there."

Paul snorted. "And how do you propose we do that?"

Billy shrugged. "I don't know yet. But we can't keep doing this forever. We need to take a chance, try to make something happen."

Paul looked at him sceptically. "And what if it doesn't work?"

Paul St John had a unique, strange attraction, his hair was dark brown with the ends dyed a vibrant red, high cheekbones with dark cold eyes. He was around the same height as Billy, five foot eight and Paul was toned though not overly muscular, but it was obvious he worked out, as his arms were strong. Whenever Paul made an appearance he created a strange presence of some kind, it was a mystery to Billy. He had a complex personality, serious and studious but he also had a dark, unpredictable side. Billy knew to watch out for him from the first time they had met. Paul was at the bar buying drinks when someone pushed in front of him. Instead of yelling or getting physically aggressive with them, he'd calmly grabbed the man by the back of the neck and slammed his face against the bar. When he'd pulled him back up, he'd seen that the poor man's nose had split open and there was blood everywhere. He simply said, "I was fucking here first" before walking away from the bar and suggesting they get their drinks somewhere else. The rest of the band had exchanged shocked looks before obediently following him.

"I'm not saying it will work," Billy interjected, "but we need to do something. We've got no money and if we don't leave this dump soon we'll be kicked out anyway. We haven't paid the rent for two months and Micky took the money that was set aside for the bills.

Micky Sinclair was the band's drummer. He was tall and muscular, with big shoulders and a head of thick black curls. His accent was unmistakably from Birmingham but his voice was surprisingly high-pitched, a stark contrast to his edgy and cool exterior. He had an infectious, jovial personality that won him friends everywhere he went, despite him being a bit of a rogue and a bit of a rebel.

Paul started, "Vince and Micky are supposed to be meeting someone this evening. Something to do with management, I didn't pay too much attention to it. But hey, maybe something good will come out of it, then I'll take more interest."

Billy felt a spark of hope ignite within him at Paul's words. "Really? Who are they meeting?" he asked, leaning forward with anticipation.

Paul shrugged. "I don't know. Some woman Vince met at a bar. But apparently she's got connections in the industry."

Billy felt excitement bubble up inside of him. This could be it, the chance they had been waiting for.

"If it works out we need to make sure we impress her," Billy said, determination shining in his eyes. "We need to show her that we're the real deal."

Paul nodded in agreement, a rare smile flickering across his face. "Yeah. Let's do it, I was bored watching this film anyway."

They grabbed their guitars from the other room and began to play. They spent hours going through the songs tweaking their set list and perfecting their sound. Billy felt a sense of purpose he hadn't felt in a long time, a drive to succeed that pushed him to work harder than ever before.

Finally, Vince and Micky arrived back at the house, grinning from ear to ear. "Guys, you won't believe it," Vince said, practically bouncing with excitement. "If we're good at the gig on Friday we've got a manager."

Vince Reid, the tall, dark frontman of The Innocents, commanded attention wherever he went. His long black hair was slicked back and his strong jawline set in a determined expression. He had ebony eyes that shone brightly in contrast to his dark skin. He wore black leather trousers, red cowboy boots, and a ripped T-shirt that exposed a rose tattoo encircling his upper left arm. He had an aura of confidence and strength that made him every inch a rock star.

Billy had met Vince many years before when he'd answered an advert in a music paper for a guitarist. Vince wasn't too impressed with him, and didn't ask him to join the band. But two years later, when Vince moved to Billy's hometown, they met again by chance in a local bar and got talking. Vince told him that he would have invited Billy to join his band back then if it hadn't been for his ginger hair! In truth, Billy had dyed his hair red and it had faded to ginger but he never gave it a second thought. There he was now all in black leather with bleached white hair looking very different from when they first met. Vince had still yet to find a second guitarist for the band so Billy joined anyway. The two of them became best friends, although Billy suspected that Vince would sell his grandmother and leave her at the side of the road if it meant he could get ahead in music, he had to admit to himself that he probably wouldn't be far behind. It seemed like they both shared this pact to drag each other up or down depending on how things went. The Innocent had been together for a year and had built up a small cult following but they felt stuck with nowhere to go. The gigs were good but they couldn't find a record deal and patience was running thin amongst them, they had argued over the best way forward, Vince and Billy had left, they recruited Micky and Paul, and they all moved down to London together where they formed a new version of The Innocent.

The band spent the next two days rehearsing non-stop, fine-tuning every detail of their set. They wanted to make sure that they were absolutely flawless for their performance on Friday night. Billy had never felt so excited before, a buzzing energy coursing through his veins. He knew that this was their chance to finally achieve their dreams of being in the music industry.

The day of the performance finally arrived, and they were at the venue early to set up their equipment and run through a final sound check. As they waited backstage for their turn to perform, Billy felt his nerves beginning to kick in. What if they screwed up? What if this woman didn't like their music? But then, as they stepped out onto the stage and the crowd started cheering, all of his doubts vanished. He felt completely in his element, playing his guitar with passion and energy. The rest of the band was on fire too, with Vince leading the way with his commanding presence and powerful vocals.

As they finished their final song and the crowd erupted into applause. They had done it, they had given a great performance and now it was up to this woman to decide if they were good enough.

The band waited nervously backstage as a mature, glamorous blond approached them, a look of contemplation on her face. She introduced herself as Sarah Morton, a music manager who said she had worked with some of the biggest bands in the industry. She told them that she had been blown away by their performance, and that she thought they had real potential.

Chapter Six

Billy's head pounded and he felt a thick fog clouding his memory. He knew that the band had wowed Sarah enough that she'd offered to manage them. The rest was a little harder to recall.

After some drinks to celebrate Vince, Paul and Sarah had left together while Billy and Micky had stayed talking to some girls at the bar. One girl named Rachel had invited Billy to go on somewhere else with her for more drinks at a club she said she could get into for free, but he couldn't recall what had happened after that. He vaguely remembered going back and having more drinks at what must have been her place. He'd stayed for a while and then he remembered getting out of bed, getting dressed and somehow making it back home without knowing how he got there. The one clear memory he did have was that they'd found themselves a manager, finally!

With that comforting thought in mind, Billy let his imagination drift. He imagined the bright lights of the stage, the roar of the crowd, and the feeling of being on top of the world. He imagined touring the world with his best friends, playing sold-out shows in huge arenas.

Then Billy's thoughts turned back to Rachel and the night before. He felt a pang of guilt mixed with a sense of excitement. He couldn't remember exactly what had happened, but he knew that he had enjoyed his time with her. Maybe this could be something more, a chance to have a real connection with someone outside of the band.

But then, just as quickly as the thought had entered his mind, it vanished. He knew that he couldn't let anything distract him from achieving his dreams. There was work to be done, and he knew that he needed to give it his all if they were going to make it. The future was uncertain, but for the first time in a long time, Billy felt like he was exactly where he was meant to be.

He slipped out of bed, dressed and clattered downstairs. He might have been exactly where he was meant to be but he was the only one who was, the house was empty! "Where the fuck is everyone?" he mumbled to himself.

At that moment the front door opened and Micky strode in with a huge grin on his face. "Morning," he said, bright as ever. "How was your night? You won't believe what happened to me; I ended up with two of those girls from our support band. Fucking hell it was...."

The phone rang in the hallway, breaking the flow of his story and Billy rushed out to answer it, it didn't ring very often so he was keen to find out if something had happened.

"How are you doing?" asked an excited Vince on the other end of the line. "You two need to get down here as soon as you can, we've got some talking to do and some plans to make, we'll meet you at Leicester Square tube. How long will you be?"

"Micky's just walked in so give us an hour, we're leaving now." said Billy as he put down the receiver.

"Who was that?" asked Micky when he returned to the kitchen.

"Vince," replied Billy, "he sounds pretty excited too, we've got to go and meet them, we'd best get moving."

Micky nodded and they both rushed out of the house and hopped on the tube to Leicester Square. Billy couldn't help but feel a sense of anticipation building in the pit of his stomach. What could Vince possibly have to tell them that was so important?

As they stepped out of the tube station, he spotted Vince and Sarah waiting for them on the corner. They looked like they had been waiting for a while, judging by the impatient expressions on their faces.

"Sorry we're late," he said as they approached them "What's going on? Where's Paul?"

"He's over there," said Vince, pointing to a coffee stand on the other side of the road. "We're going to go back to Sarah's, we've got some news."

They all marched across to Piccadilly and up into Eagle Place where Sarah had a top floor apartment. They filed out of the lift and she opened the front door. The living room was filled with the bright morning sunlight coming in from the balcony, highlighting the expensive kitchen appliances, full wine rack, and marble worktops. An empty bottle of wine lay on its side next to a half eaten bag of dry roasted nuts and two used glasses on the sink unit. At the other end of the living room an open bedroom door revealed tangled bed covers on the floor, hinting at more than just conversation between Sarah and Vince the night before.

Billy tried to ignore the sight and focused his attention on Sarah, who was already starting to speak.

"Listen up, boys," she said, her voice full of enthusiasm. "Last night was just the beginning. We've got a lot of work to do, but I believe we can take this band to the next level. I'm going to get a few gigs lined up over the next few weeks, but that's just the start. I've been in touch this morning with a producer friend of mine, Justin Hickman. Vince and I are meeting him and his wife later to play some of your stuff. If he thinks he can improve anything then we'll get to work on some more tracks and get you in the studio."

Micky let out a whoop of excitement while Billy sat

there, stunned. This was all happening so fast. They had barely finished recording their demo. But he knew that this was the chance of a lifetime, and he was determined to make the most of it.

About an hour later they left Sarah's apartment and headed into Soho for a celebration drink. "Did you shag her?" asked Micky with a big smile on his face.

"I had to mate, I didn't have anywhere to go," replied Vince defensively. "I thought I was going to sleep on the sofa but she just jumped on me and dragged me into her bedroom."

"Bet you put up a real fucking fight," grunted Paul, "Still, if we can get something out of it before you get bored and fuck her off then I don't suppose it matters does it?"

"Let's just concentrate on getting some recording done with a top producer shall we," retorted Vince. "Let's go to The Ship and decide what we're going to do."

They walked into The Ship on Wardour Street, it was an old fashioned London pub, with a tiled green floor and an oak, wood panelled bar that was popular with the music executives from the many record companies in the area. They bought drinks, sat at a table at the end of the bar and set about discussing what songs to record.

Three large, overweight figures sat on barstools about six feet away, drawing on cigars and drinking gin and tonic from fancy highball glasses. Billy recognised two of them as Martin Kerry, the head of a large publishing company who had offered to publish some of their songs until the other figure he knew, Antony Weston Davies, the head of Lost Sanctuary Records had interjected and said there were many better artists around than this bunch, "They're just another band from up north!" he'd said dismissively. Kerry had withdrawn his offer, to go away and have a think about it and nothing had been said since. Billy and Vince had assumed that it was all dead in the water and by the lack of recognition as they all sat there, it seemed that that was still the case.

The third figure, who Billy didn't know, looked over at them and smiled. It was a horrible, letching smile and they quickly looked away and continued their conversation. This was no time to become involved with three old queens looking for some entertainment on a Saturday afternoon.

The band drank quickly and left the pub, Vince left them in Soho and started off back to Sarah's apartment ready for the meeting with Justin and his wife.

"Let us know how it goes," shouted Paul as Vince disappeared around a corner.

"I'm going home," said Billy, "I can't afford to stay out all day," He turned and slowly walked off up the road to Oxford Street to get the tube.

"We'll see you later then," said Micky, and he and

Paul went off in the other direction in search of some more entertainment.

Billy found a seat on the sweaty, crowded train platform, waiting for his tube and an escape from the heat. He was looking forward to getting home and writing some music. Partying and chasing women seemed fun when he was drunk or out of his head on drugs but this wasn't the life he wanted. Instead, he craved nothing more than playing live, writing music and putting in hours in the studio. It was what made him feel alive! He couldn't stand the pretentiousness of London's music scene. All he wanted was someone real, not just some casual fling that changed each night or every month depending on who was doing what.

He shook himself out of the negativity that had clung to him on the way home and picked up his guitar, he hoped for some good news from Vince later, but until then he would lose himself in his world of music.

Chapter Seven

Vince arrived back at Sarah's apartment with a sense of nervousness. Meeting with Justin Hickman could be just the break that the band needed, but it could also be a disappointment. He knocked on the door, and Sarah answered with a smile. "He's here," she said, stepping aside to let Vince in.

Justin Hickman and his wife Alicia were already there, sitting on the sofa. The couple looked like they were in their mid-forties, Justin was a round-faced individual with an Asian appearance. He looked sharp in his black suit and luxury snakeskin cowboy boots. Beside him was his stunning wife, Alicia Moran, her bright red hair cascading down around her striking green eyes. She wore a dark suit with an elegant skirt that ended just above the knee and heels to show off her curves. Her fame as one of the members of an all-girl band that had produced a couple of top ten hits preceded her. They both smiled broadly when Vince entered and shook his hand enthusiastically.

Vince felt a little intimidated by their presence but pushed the feeling aside. This was his chance to show what he and his band were capable of.

They chatted for a while before Sarah moved to the expensive music centre in a corner of the room and played their demo.

Justin listened intently, nodding his head along with the beat. When it finished, he turned to Vince. "I like it," he said, "It's raw, but there's potential there."

Vince breathed a sigh of relief. Maybe this was it, the chance to break out of the underground scene and into the mainstream.

"Let's get started then," said Justin, standing up and brushing off his suit. "I've got a studio booked for next month. We'll start with a couple of your songs and see where we can take them."

Vince felt the excitement rising within him. This was what he had dreamed of, making music with a legend like Justin Hickman. He thanked him and his wife as they left, leaving Vince practically skipping around Sarah's apartment.

"Can I use your phone?" he asked excitedly. "I've got to call Billy and let him know."

"Yeah, sure," Sarah replied, and Vince picked up the phone and dialled the house number.

Billy was sat in the kitchen with his guitar when he heard the phone ring. He had an idea who it'd be and he was right. It was Vince.

"It's all happening mate!" Vince gushed down the line, "Justin wants to record some of our songs!"

"That's brilliant," said Billy, "What are we going to record?"

"He wants to start with a couple of our best ones and see how we get on. There could be a record deal in it for us mate! It could be our big break!"

"Fucking Hell! I can't wait to hear the results. Have you told Paul and Micky?"

"No, I went straight to Sarah's for the meeting after I left you at the pub. I haven't seen Micky or Paul since."

"No problem," said Billy. "I suppose they'll come back when their money runs out. Will you be here tonight or are you going to stay at Sarah's again?"

"No, I'm coming back," Vince whispered, looking around to make sure she wasn't listening in on the conversation. "I think it's better not to get too involved in this. I'm just going to have a quick drink with her here before coming back. We need to plan everything out before the others get back."

"All right then, see you soon," said Billy as his mind started spinning with ideas. He put the phone down and grabbed his guitar. "I'm going to make sure these songs turn out as best as we can get them," he muttered before diving back into his own little world.

A few hours later, Vince strolled in through the door and shouted out, trying to make Billy hear him above the music in his headphones.

"You what mate?" Billy questioned, taking them off.

"I've got more news," Vince repeated. "Sarah made a few phone calls while I was there. I don't know how many people she actually knows but it seems she's well connected, she kept on mentioning that a couple of them owed her a favour. Anyway, we can play some gigs, one on the 14th and the other on the 20th. We should definitely do those because there's a chance for us to be a support act at The Marquee towards the end of the month for an Australian band on their first tour here. Apparently they're going to be massive so it'll be packed. Sarah said she'd let us know tomorrow if it works out."

Billy couldn't contain his excitement. "Fucking hell mate that's amazing. This is really coming together isn't it? We need to get our rehearsals sorted out so we can do these gigs, then get straight into the studio, we'll sound tight as ever. I'll call the rehearsal room tomorrow and book us in for the week."

"That's great Billy," said Vince. "What are you writing? Anything good?"

"I'm working on something new," he said, strumming his guitar. "I've got a sort of chorus idea."

"Well, play it for me," encouraged Vince.

Billy didn't need any more encouragement. He pressed play on his cassette player and played along with the new song he'd been working on. Vince listened intently as the sound filled the kitchen. He felt goose bumps rising on his arms as Billy played and he started to hum a melody along with it. Before long they'd got the rough outline of a brand new song.

"Billy, that's good," Vince said as he ended the song. "That's really good."

"Thanks mate," Billy replied, "but we always seem to work well when we bounce ideas off each other, we don't do it enough but I guess we're going to have to work a bit harder now. You fancy a drink? I could do with one."

"A beer would be good, I'm parched," Vince replied as Billy pulled two bottles from the fridge.

He poured two glasses and handed one to Vince, who immediately gulped it down.

As they sat there in the kitchen, Billy started talking about a girl he'd been seeing but who'd left him for another guy.

"I'm over it now," he said, taking a swig of his beer. "I've got my music to focus on, and I've got you guys."

"Yeah," Vince replied, feeling a twinge of guilt. He had been secretly seeing this girl on and off for the past month. He knew it was wrong, but he couldn't help himself.

"I'm glad we're doing this," Billy said, interrupting Vince's thoughts. "I've always felt like we could be something special, you know?"

"Yeah," Vince agreed, feeling a sudden surge of

emotion. "I feel the same way. We've got something good going on here."

They clinked their glasses together and continued talking late into the night, planning their future and dreaming of success. But as Vince lay in bed later that night, he couldn't shake the guilt he felt about Billy's ex-girlfriend. He knew he had to tell him the truth, even if it meant risking their friendship and their music.

The next day, Vince went down to the kitchen, his heart pounding in his chest. He knew he had to come clean about the girl he'd been seeing, and he wasn't sure how Billy was going to react.

Billy was making himself a cup of tea and Vince could see the excitement in his eyes. "Mate, you won't believe it," Billy said. "Sarah just called, and we're playing at The Marquee as the support act for that Australian band!"

Vince felt the relief wash over him. He'd been so worried about telling Billy the truth, but now he realised that they had more important things to worry about. "That's amazing, Billy," he said, smiling. "We're going to have put some work in though, are the others back yet?

"Micky's in bed but Paul didn't come home."

As soon as the words had left his mouth Paul strode in with a troubled look on his face. "

"Where the fuck have you been?" Asked Vince, smiling, "You've missed it all mate, it's great news."

"I know all about it," said Paul, grateful for the distraction. "I couldn't get back last night as I'd missed the last tube. I went to Sarah's flat and she let me stay. She told me about the gigs, it's great isn't it?"

They spent the rest of the day rehearsing, going over the new songs they'd written and practising their old ones. Billy was in high spirits, and Vince knew that he had made the right decision in keeping his secret to himself. They were a team, and nothing could come between them.

As the days passed, the band continued to rehearse and prepare for their upcoming gigs. Vince couldn't help but feel proud of how far they had come. They were on the brink of playing at one of the most iconic venues in London. But despite their success, Vince couldn't shake the guilt he felt, he knew he had to tell Billy the truth, but every time he tried to bring it up, something always got in the way.

It wasn't until the day of their first gig that Vince finally found the courage to come clean.

As they were loading their equipment into the van, Vince pulled Billy aside and took a deep breath.

"There's something I need to tell you," he said, his voice shaking slightly.

Billy looked at him expectantly, waiting for him to continue.

"It's about that girl you were seeing," Vince said,

finally getting the words out. "The one who left you for another guy."

Billy's eyes narrowed in confusion. "Yeah, what about her?"

Vince took another deep breath. "I've been seeing her too," he admitted.

Billy's face fell. "You what?"

"I know it's wrong, and I'm sorry," Vince said quickly. "I should have told you sooner, but I didn't want to ruin our friendship or the band."

Billy looked shocked, "You've got to be fucking kidding me!" he exclaimed, his face a mix of surprise and disbelief. "I can't believe you didn't fucking tell me about this. I was trying to talk to her, but she kept avoiding me. If I had known earlier, I wouldn't have made myself look like a fucking idiot would I? I liked her, but I'm not going to keep chasing after her. You can have her mate, she's all yours."

He wanted to appear unaffected, but inside he was hurting. It wasn't the fact that she'd gone off with Vince that upset him; it was the fact that she hadn't told him she was doing so which hurt most of all. He had really liked her too, another example of one of his bad experiences with women, he thought to himself.

They drove in a dark blue transit van to the Half Moon, a renowned music venue tucked away in a Fulham alleyway. After taking in the sight of its graffiti-covered walls and feeling the sticky carpets, they quickly unloaded their equipment and set up on an impressively sized stage. The stale smell of beer and cigarettes permeated the air, but this was nothing new for them, they were used to playing dive bars and iconic venues alike. Their minds filled with nostalgia as they took in the history that hung thickly in the atmosphere. This was going to be a good gig.

After sound check Billy took himself off to a small bar over the road from the Half Moon, he got himself a drink and sat in the corner, lighting up a cigarette. He thought about the girl and Vince. He took a drag on his cigarette and exhaled deeply, he had gone through a lot of bad luck with women over the years. He thought back to the girls at school, the ones who'd teased him mercilessly.

He remembered how, on his first day at middle school, his mum had thought it would be a good idea to send him in shorts. All the other boys wore long trousers, and there he was with his scrawny white legs out for everyone to see. His classmates began calling him "Cream" because of his fair skin, then "Cream Puff" before eventually escalating to "Gay Boy" and "Queer". The girls had joined in taunting him, and it went on like this for years. Eventually, as he became recognised for his sports skills and musical talent, the jeers turned into admiration. But by then, it was too late, the damage had been done and he developed an aversion towards certain types of women.

He had lost his virginity to a girl called Diana Lawrence; she was two years older than him and nick-named "Tiger". They'd been at a house party and found themselves in the bedroom, among piles of coats and jackets. It was frantic and over in an instant, leaving them quickly going their separate ways. Billy hadn't realised why Diana had her nickname until he saw the long scratches down his back and shoulders the morning after. He had tried to ignore it in the pub when he heard her and her friends laughing about it, but all he could do was leave before anyone noticed his humiliation.

Diana wouldn't be the last girl to hurt him, and he had learnt to be very cautious with his feelings for women. He had settled down since he'd joined the band, not believing in love because it had hurt him too many times before, but truth be told, he was starting to feel lonely.

He finished his drink and went back over to the Half Moon, he thought about the new songs they had been rehearsing, and how much fun it was to play them. He was a bit jealous that Vince had written the lyrics and melodies, but at the end of the day he still knew that they wouldn't be where they were today without him. Billy decided that he would try to make up with Vince. He was a good mate; they'd get over it.

He walked through the main room, which was filling

up nicely. He made his way backstage and found Vince in the dressing room, "You ok?" he asked. "Yes mate, all good," Billy replied and gave Vince a hug.

"You lot look fucking great," he said, "I'd best get myself changed." and he dug about in his bag and started unpacking.

He dressed in tight black leather trousers that fitted him perfectly, tucked into his favourite cowboy boots, he put on a faded green vest underneath a silk black shirt with flecks of silver, it was open to his waist. Around his neck he wore a leather rope necklace and a silver chain that was given to him by his mum on his eightieth birthday. There were small-hooped gold earrings in both ears and an assortment of silver and leather bangles on each wrist.

"Where's the mirror?" he asked, looking around.

"Couldn't find one in here," replied Paul, "you have to use the one in the toilets in the main bar."

Billy made his way to the toilets at the front of the public bar and checked himself out in the mirror, messing about with his hair. He was applying his black eyeliner when a sturdy looking man walked in, obviously very drunk. The man went to the full-length urinal and unzipped his trousers. Billy had grown to hate these cramped places, knowing that someone else's piss would splash onto his boots whenever the place was packed. As he turned to leave, the man was standing watching him, his trousers and zipper still open; he stepped closer and grabbed at Billy's crotch with a dirty, fat hand. Billy felt an uneasiness rise at the unwelcome contact. He responded by pushing back against the man's chest, before delivering a perfect palm strike to his forehead. The man stumbled, knocked off balance and fell into the sink units behind him. Without wasting time, Billy made a break for it back to the safety of the dressing room and his friends.

"What the fuck's happened to you?" asked Micky as he stumbled back into the room looking a little panicked and flustered.

"Just another little incident with a drunken gentleman in the toilets," he said, trying to make light of it.

"Fuck me, you don't help yourself dressed like that do you? Not in a bar like that anyway," said Micky with a huge smile on his face.

Billy turned and put some things back in his bag, relieved that he'd managed to get away unscathed.

He liked to get into the music and disassociate himself from his surroundings, and tonight was no different. He quickly forgot about the incident in the toilet and he was feeling good about himself. Vince shouted out with enthusiasm as the intro music began to play and the members of the band grabbed their instruments. Billy could feel the energy from the crowd, and Micky set off a thunderous rhythm on the drums. As the lights illuminated the stage, Billy was in his element; this was all he had ever wanted.

They were off to a good start, and the gig was almost sold out. They played a great set, and the crowd loved it. They knew they were a good band, and Billy couldn't help but feel some sense of satisfaction when they left the stage to a standing ovation.

Chapter Eight

Billy woke with a start, disoriented and unsure of where he was. He glanced to his right and saw a mass of tangled blond locks. He closed his eyes and tried to remember what had happened the night before.

They had played a great show, and Sarah had proposed they go into town. They had ended up at The Embassy, a fashionable club in Bond Street where Sarah's acquaintance (at least that's what she called him) had been incredibly generous with his cocaine. Billy vaguely recalled sniffing it off a tiny silver spoon in the toilets and swigging from a vodka bottle being passed around their table. How much did he have?

His head pounded as he looked around, it was an opulent bedroom with a high ceiling and floor-to-ceiling glass wardrobes down one side. He knew that he was in a plush flat somewhere in London, but he had no idea where, he couldn't remember how he'd got there. He squeezed his eyes shut as a wave of nausea hit him. The woman lying next to him stirred and let out a soft moan. He tried to remember her name; he'd taken so much cocaine that it was impossible to recall it at that moment. He rolled away from her and sat up on the edge of the bed, Billy stood up and walked over to the full-length mirror by the wall. He felt sick as he saw his reflection, a sunken face with bloodshot eyes. His shoulders were rounded, and his stomach looked bloated. His hair was dishevelled and smeared with make-up. He was disgusted with himself.

He looked around for his clothes and found his vest, trousers and boots. God knows where his shirt was but he couldn't be arsed to look for it. He dressed and left the bedroom without a sound. He found himself in a large hallway with a black and white tiled floor, posters of fashion models lined one wall, and on the opposite side of the hall there stood a coat stand and mirror framed with a hand-carved border. He went out through the front door, making sure to close it silently before he made his way to the sweeping staircase, which led him down to the hall and street level outside. Cold October air filled his lungs as he stepped out into the cold morning. He looked around, his gaze finding Holland Park tube station. He began walking towards it, shivering in the faded green vest he'd been wearing since the gig last night. Fumbling through his pockets for change, he found nothing. With a sigh of resignation, he jumped over the ticket barriers and sprinted to the platform. Luckily, there wasn't a guard on duty but he knew that wouldn't be the case when he tried to leave at the other end. He made his way down the steps and towards the platform; the air was full of dust from the train that had just pulled in. He squeezed through the crowd; still paralysed by the vodka and cocaine hangover he'd woken up with. He plunged himself down on a seat as the train lurched forward and he felt another wave of nausea hit him.

He got out at Wood Green station before jumping the barriers again; he headed down the high street towards home. As he walked, Billy tried to piece together what had happened the night before. He remembered the gig and the crowds, the music and the energy. But everything else was a blur. He had no idea who the woman was, or how he had ended up in her bed. He had no memory of leaving the club, or getting into a taxi, or anything else that might have led him to this moment. All he knew was that he felt like shit, and he needed to get home.

As he turned down his street, he could see his house at the end of the road. He quickened his pace, eager to get home and crawl back into bed. He opened the front door and stepped inside, the familiar smell of stale cigarette smoke and beer washing over him. He made his way up the stairs to his room, and as he pushed open the door, he saw that his bed was unmade and his clothes were strewn across the floor. He let out a deep sigh and sat down on the edge of the bed. He knew he should clean up, but the thought of moving made him feel sick. He lay down, fully clothed, and closed his eyes. He woke up a few hours later, feeling slightly more coherent. He got up and began to straighten up his room, trying to push the nagging feeling of self-disgust out of his mind.

He took a long hot shower, hoping it would help clear his head. As he stood under the steaming water, memories of the woman from the night before came flooding back. He tried to focus on something else, but his mind wouldn't let him. He wondered if he would ever see her again, and if he did, would he even remember her name?

He got dressed and headed down to the kitchen, where Micky was cooking some bacon. "You look like shit," He said as Billy walked in.

"Yeah, thanks for that," Billy muttered, grabbing a cup of tea and sitting down at the table.

"What happened last night?" Micky asked, eyeing him suspiciously. "You disappeared with some girl, didn't even say goodbye."

Billy sighed. "I don't remember much after we left the club. I woke up in her bed this morning, and I couldn't even remember her name."

Micky raised an eyebrow. "Sounds like you had a good night then."

"Fucking hell mate don't," said Billy quietly, "I've got to stop...."

"Bollocks," yelled Paul as soon as he stepped into the kitchen, disrupting their chat. "That was our landlord on the telephone. He wants us to be out of here by Friday."

"What did we do?" asked Micky.

"Well, I think it's because we haven't paid any rent for four months and you've 'borrowed' most of the money needed for the bills. The neighbours on both sides have also complained about all the chaos and noise coming from this house, so I suppose he has a little trouble with us living here. What do you think?" Paul said sarcastically.

"Where are we going to go?" spluttered Micky.

Billy sat in silence, his mind racing with a million thoughts. He knew that their situation was dire, they were all struggling to make ends meet and were constantly behind on rent and bills. It was only a matter of time before they were kicked out and left to fend for themselves on the streets.

"We'll sort it out," Billy said, trying to sound confident. "We always do."

As they sat around the kitchen table, trying to come up with a plan, Vince appeared through the back door. "Morning," he said confidently, "what's going on?"

"We're been kicked out on Friday, you got any ideas," grunted Paul.

"Why do you always look to me for ideas when shit

happens," countered Vince, annoyed that his good mood had just been shattered.

"I'm not asking you to sort it out," Paul said slightly too aggressively. "I was just asking if you had any ideas."

"You've got your brother in Brixton haven't you?" said Vince nodding at Micky and quickly diffusing the situation, "You and Paul could stop there for a few days and me and Billy could sort something else out. It won't be for long and it'll give us a bit of breathing space to all get ourselves sorted out. We shouldn't all be living together anyway, we need our own space."

Micky nodded in agreement, grateful that Vince always seemed to have a solution to their problems. "Yeah, that could work," he said. "Thanks, I'll call him and see if he's okay with us crashing there for a few days."

Paul grumbled something under his breath, but didn't say anything else. They all knew that they needed to do something, and fast.

Billy, always the optimist, suggested that they should get back to rehearsing for the gig at The Marquee. This conversation seemed to finally give them a purpose and a focus. They agreed that this was their best bet, and if all went well they would be able to concentrate on finding themselves places to live as well as replace Sarah as manager.

Vince wanted her out since he suspected that she was treating them as some sort of toy. She was well known in the music world and had a few connections, though people seemed to find her antics a bit of a joke. After her divorce she'd received a large sum of money and had begun to take on young bands, she'd sometimes have inappropriate contact with one or two members and she was known for giving them grand promises before eventually discarding them. Vince knew she had recently seen Paul alone overnight, confirming what he'd heard about her.

"We need to be careful how we approach getting rid of her," he said "I think we should keep quiet until after The Marquee gig just in case she pulls us out of it."

"Definitely," agreed Billy, "we can't afford to mess up this chance."

They discussed who could take over from Sarah. After a few hours of deliberation, they eventually agreed on Alicia Moran, she wasn't just an ex-pop star and Justin Hickman's wife. She was an experienced music manager based in London. She had already made a name for herself in the industry, and was known for her ability to get the best out of the bands she managed.

They all agreed to focus on rehearsing for the upcoming gig at The Marquee, and they worked hard over the following days to make sure they were ready.

Micky and Paul decided it was time to move into his brother's place in Brixton. They knew he'd take them in for a short while, and they'd be able to sort themselves out during that time.

Micky called his brother, who was more than happy

to help out. He welcomed them with open arms, and said he had plenty of room for them both to stay. Micky thanked him sincerely before hanging up the phone.

Paul let out a long sigh of relief, now at least their immediate accommodation issue was sorted!

The next thing on their agenda was to get in touch with Alicia Moran. Billy suggested that Vince should go and speak to her, as he was the one who indirectly knew her through Justin Hickman.

Vince agreed but thought it would be a good idea if Billy came along, so the two of them made their way towards the tube station, grabbed a train ticket and headed straight for Sloane Square, excited for what the future might bring. When they arrived, they found themselves outside of Alicia's office building. Vince pushed his nerves aside and took a deep breath before heading inside.

He knocked on the door and waited anxiously as he heard footsteps from within before it opened to reveal a glamorous woman with bright red hair wearing an expensive looking tailored suit. "Vince," she said with a smile, her accent carrying a soft Irish lilt. "Come in, I'm intrigued to hear what you want to talk to me about."

Vince introduced Billy and explained why they were there. She listened carefully as Vince told her about his plans for her managing the band.

"That would put me in a very awkward position," Alicia said thoughtfully, "Sarah is a good friend of mine as you know but business is business so I'm prepared to think about it."

She wanted to hear them live first so Vince invited her to come to The Marquee gig in two weeks time, promising that it would be a fantastic show!

Alicia accepted his offer and said that she'd bring Justin along so he could hear the songs played live before they went into the studio. If everything went well she'd find a way of clearing everything with Sarah but there were no promises. If she thought they were good enough then, she'd get involved.

Billy and Vince left and walked off up the Kings Road to find somewhere they could have a celebratory drink happy in the knowledge that they would move on to the next stage of their careers if, and it was a big if, they did themselves justice at The Marquee. In the meantime, they had the small matter of finding somewhere to live.

Chapter Nine

Billy and Vince were sitting in a bar near the Kings Road in Chelsea when Billy suddenly recalled that one of their roadies had a cousin who did home renovations.

"That's brilliant!" Vince exclaimed, "Give him a call and ask if he can help us out."

Billy reached into his pocket for some coins and made his way to the payphone at the end of the bar. A few minutes later, he returned with a wide grin on his face.

"Jimmy says his cousin is doing up a place in Finsbury Park at the moment. He's not sure what sort of state it's in but he said he'd give him a call and let us know later. I'll phone him back about six and find out."

The two of them sat and talked through some ideas for the band for the next couple of hours before phoning Jimmy back and arranging to see the place they were going to stay at. Jimmy said he'd meet them there later that evening so after grabbing their bags from back at their house, they took another train journey towards Finsbury Park before eventually arriving outside a terraced house on Seven Sisters Road.

"It looks ok," said Vince, as they stood outside waiting.

Five minutes later Jimmy walked up with a set of keys in his hand.

"You can stay for three days," he said "then the builders are back to do some more work so you'll need to be out by then."

"No worries," replied Billy, "we should be able to find somewhere else to stay by then."

Jimmy opened the door and the three of them walked inside, it was far from what they expected. At first glance, Billy and Vince were both disappointed. The place was a complete building site with nothing but concrete floors, bare walls and a few exposed pipes here and there. The entire room smelt of fresh plaster and the air was thick with dust particles that hung in front of their faces like sheets in the stillness of the night. It wasn't exactly what they had been expecting but, with no other option available to them, they decided to make do for the night at least.

Jimmy showed them around and explained where the shower was located before leaving them alone as he walked away into the night. Even though it was cold inside, neither of them fancied going back out onto the streets to find somewhere else so they opened up their sleeping bags on either side of the living room floor and got ready to try and get some sleep.

When the sun rose, they were still awake on the hard concrete floor, shivering from the cold. Neither of them had got any rest, but Billy had an idea for a different place they could stay. He'd remembered that a distant cousin of his mums had suggested that if he ever needed anywhere to stay then he should give her a call. It had been around five years since she'd made the offer, Billy had been at a family gathering and Irene, the lady in question, had been talking to him. She was in her early fifties but she was a nice enough lady, fairly average looking and single since her divorce. She'd been very interested in Billy's plan to move to London and follow his dreams and she'd given him a phone number and told him to call her if he ever needed any help. She lived in Romford which was a fair way out of London but if they could stay there for a couple of days it wouldn't matter too much.

"You've got to give her a call mate," pleaded Vince, "If we stay another night here I'm not sure we'll survive, I'm fucking freezing."

"I know," Billy replied, "let's go and get some breakfast and get warm and I'll see if I can find her number."

They found a cafe and grabbed a quick breakfast before he found Irene's number and, after taking a deep breath, he dialled it hoping for the best. It was a couple of rings before she answered.

"Hello?" Irene asked, "Who's calling?"

"Hi, it's me, Billy Maguire," said Billy nervously. "You may not remember me but we met at one of my mum's family gatherings about five years ago. You said that if I ever needed help then I should give you a call.

"Of course I remember you," said Irene, "how are you?"

"Listen I'm sorry to bother you but I was wondering if there was any chance that my friend Vince and I could stay with you for a couple of days? We're in London at the moment and we don't really have anywhere else to go."

Irene agreed to let them stay for a few nights while they looked for another place. She instructed them to catch a train out to Romford. Billy thanked Irene profusely before saying goodbye and hanging up the phone. He was relieved with this new stroke of luck; their situation had suddenly become much better!

"We're sorted mate," whispered Billy excitedly "Irene is going to take us in for a few days until we find some-where else."

Billy and Vince caught the train to Romford. Upon arriving at Irene's house they were surprised at her appearance. She wore bright green high heels to match her tight-fitting dress that hugged her slim figure perfectly. She opened the door and greeted them with a warm hug; they couldn't help but be taken aback by her vibrant energy and stylishness given her age.

Walking into the house felt like walking into an oasis of calm. It was exquisitely decorated with beautiful furniture and art from every corner of the world. Irene led them to their room, where she'd already prepared two single beds that were separated only by a gorgeous glass floor lamp standing in the middle of the room. The beds themselves were adorned with soft white sheets that were so comfortable you could sink right in.

Irene then showed them around the rest of the house, there was a spacious living room filled with brightly coloured rugs and plush sofas, an old-fashioned kitchen decked out with classic appliances and even a library stocked full of books on every subject imaginable!

"Make yourselves at home," she said, "are you hungry?"

"No we're good thanks," said Billy, "Thank you so much for this, you wouldn't believe where we spent last night."

"I can only imagine," Irene said with a knowing smile. She chuckled and said not to worry about it, she was happy to help them out. They chatted for a while then Irene's daughter and her boyfriend came back. They were very suspicious of the two friends and questioned them why they've phoned out of the blue and asked to stay. Irene then intervened and told them their story but they didn't seem satisfied. The atmosphere was tense for the remainder of the afternoon, but then Irene declared she was taking Vince and Billy out for drinks that night to meet a few of her friends.

Billy and Vince got changed into something more presentable and went to wait in the living room. Irene appeared wearing a short leopard print dress and very high heels, she looked like somebody who worked in a questionable cocktail bar! She had applied heavy make-up around her eyes and was wearing a pair of dangling earrings that moved when she spoke.

"Let's go," said Irene with a wink, "we've got some other friends meeting us there, so we'd better not be late."

Vince and Billy looked at each other not knowing what they had let themselves in for, but followed Irene out of the door anyway. They walked for a few minutes until they arrived at a trendy bar that was bustling with activity. Irene led them through the crowds of people and over to a table where a group of her friends were already sitting.

"Guys, this is Billy and Vince," Irene introduced them, "they're staying with me for a few days while they find their feet in London."

The group greeted them warmly and they all began to chat and drink together. Billy and Vince were surprised at how friendly and open Irene's friends were, given their initial reception from Irene's daughter and boyfriend. The night went by in a blur of laughter and alcohol, with the group moving from one bar to another until the early hours of the morning.

As they walked back to Irene's house, they were all laughing and joking together. Billy and Vince couldn't believe how much their luck had changed in such a short space of time. They were grateful to Irene for taking them in and introducing them to her friends.

"I hope you guys had fun tonight," Irene said as they arrived home, "I know my friends can be a bit much sometimes but they mean well."

"We had fun, thanks for taking us out," said Vince, grinning from ear to ear.

"It was my pleasure," Irene said as she took Vince's hand and led him out of the room.

Billy sat on the sofa, his head swimming from all the alcohol trying to focus on the books up on the shelf to his right.

Irene returned to the room alone, a big smile on her face.

"Feeling adventurous, Billy?" She asked him, a mischievous glint in her eye"

I...I don't know," he stammered nervously.

"Oh, come on," Irene said, moving closer to him, "don't be shy, trust me I can be a lot of fun."

Billy hesitated for a moment, and then heard Vince snoring from the other room. It was just him and Irene now.

Billy woke the next morning. Everything was slowly

coming back to him as he began to piece together what had happened the night before. After being taken in by Irene, they'd gone out for drinks with her friends. But then everything after that was... blurry?

A light scent hung in the air that made him feel a sudden wave of discomfort—he immediately recognised it as Irene's perfume from last night. He had been sitting on the sofa looking at books while she had disappeared off into another room with Vince, she'd returned alone a couple of minutes later and sat very close to him touching his thigh...What had happened? As much as he wanted these memories not to be true, there was something inside telling him that indeed, they were real.

Taking a deep breath, Billy decided it would be best not to think about it any longer and instead tried focusing on when Vince would wake up so they could leave this place safe and sound without encountering any further embarrassing moments. As if on cue Vince rushed through the doorway looking dishevelled yet strangely happy.

"Fucking hell mate, my head hurts," said Vince quietly, "she took me to her room last night and gave a pill of some sort, it completely knocked me out."

"Yeah?" said Billy, embarrassed by what had happened. "She gave me a blow job!"

"You're joking," replied Vince, a look of disbelief on his face.

"No mate, she's crazy, we need to leave here now."

"I'm not going anywhere else yet mate, we've got to sort something out before we leave here. Just one more night and we'll go tomorrow ok?"

Billy nodded, not wanting to disagree with his friend. As much as he wanted to forget the night before and get out of there as soon as possible, he also knew that they were in a bit of a sticky situation and it would be best to stay and buy some time.

That evening, Irene shamelessly reversed their roles and took Vince to her room while Billy stayed downstairs.

The following day, they packed their bags and made their escape from Irene's house. Once they were safe outside, they breathed a sigh of relief. While their experience with Irene was nothing short of bizarre, it had taught them many valuable lessons. They both realised that they had to stay alert and trust their gut, especially when it came to strangers. With this newfound knowledge, they continued their journey, hoping never to meet anyone as strange as Irene ever again.

Chapter Ten

Billy and Vince walked out of Kentish Town tube station having made their way back into London, they were both relieved and happy that they had survived the ordeal of a couple of nights at Irene's home.

They walked north up the high street for what seemed like ages until they arrived at Archway Tower, the DHSS building where they could apply for emergency housing. Billy was very pissed off when he looked across the road and saw another tube station and realised they could have saved themselves a couple of miles walk by staying on the train for two more stops!

After climbing the stairs to the 10th floor, explaining their situation and then been made to wait for five hours, the housing officer, a grey haired lady in her early sixties, was very sympathetic and offered them a cheap hotel to stay in for a while until something more permanent could be found. They gratefully accepted and began making arrangements for their stay.

They were directed to The Queens Hotel on Queens Avenue in Muswell Hill, a very grand sounding place but how different the reality was! The room smelt of stale air and cigarette smoke but it seemed a fair exchange for the comfort and security that it offered. The walls were painted beige with an occasional dirt smudge here and there, but overall it was surprisingly well kept. A tiny window allowed the light of the day in, which illuminated the otherwise dank atmosphere. As they unpacked their belongings, Billy noticed some cobwebs in the corner but decided not to mention them to his friend as he could already sense that Vince seemed quite content with their accommodation regardless of its minimal aesthetic appeal.

The next morning they woke, and stepped into the breakfast room. It was downstairs in the basement, and consisted of eight tables each covered in cheap red and white striped tablecloths. A single rose was set in a slim vase on one table, its petals billowed outward like a balle-rina's skirt, it didn't fit in at all. The ceiling pressed down low, close to their heads, creating a very cramped envi-ronment. Self-service containers lined the far wall, and emitted a sizzle of bacon above the stench of grease and fat. At one table, a man with floppy hair was shovelling scrambled eggs into his mouth as quickly as he could, at another, a large man with a black beanie hat sat hunched over a mug of steaming tea, reading the tabloids. They found a table in the corner away from all the others and sat down. They both ordered a full English breakfast each and a pot of tea, neither of them knowing if another meal would be on offer later.

The two of them ate quickly then Billy went to the payphone in the lobby. He dialled Micky's brother's number and Paul answered in his gruff Birmingham drawl, they spoke for a while then confirmed they'd meet at the rehearsal room around noon.

Billy went back to the room to collect his guitar then he and Vince left for the bus stop, with Vince complaining about ending up in one of the few areas in London with no tube station. Billy reminded him that they had somewhere to stay, and it was an incentive to make sure they did well at The Marquee so they wouldn't have to stay there much longer. When they reached Euston Road, they got off the bus and walked down to Kings Cross to their rehearsal room at The Depot Studios. It wasn't the best place, but it was pass-able and the sound quality was ok. Micky and Paul were already set up when they arrived. "You're late," moaned Paul, "what kept you?"

"It's the buses," replied Vince with a beaming smile, "we waited for ages then two came along at once!"

The four of them played together for hours and worked tirelessly on each part until it was perfect. No details were overlooked either, tempos were improved upon, harmonies were tweaked, dynamics changed, nothing was left untouched until each song flowed better than it had before. Throughout all this practice they experienced genuine joy at simply being able to play music together, something they hadn't been able to do for what had seemed like ages.

Finally, tired but content, Billy and Vince took a bus back towards Muswell Hill, Micky and Paul disappeared into the depths of Kings Cross tube station. They watched unfamiliar street names pass by outside before arriving at their destination. As they passed through the busy streets back towards their hotel they both knew that tomorrow would be another exciting day playing music once again.

Everyday for the next two weeks, they practised the same routine over and over, committing it to memory. Billy chose to stay in most nights but Vince couldn't bear life in the hotel. He went out every night and usually stayed away until early morning.

Following their last practice, the group decided to go out in Soho and enjoy the night. It had been a while since they had all gone out together, so this seemed like a perfect opportunity for them to take some time away from the rehearsal studio and unwind. They went to The Ship, drinking beer and talking about everything and anything. Vince's stories kept them entertained with his larger than life tales of adventure and mischief, they went from bar to bar, exploring the nightlife of Soho. As the night wore on they found themselves in The Intrepid Fox, a double floored bar in Wardour Street.

The music was loud and vibrant and it seemed like every single person was dancing or moving. Micky and Vince exchanged knowing glances before joining in; even Paul couldn't resist the pull of the music and started jumping around. Billy stood watching his friends, a smile on his face as he saw them enjoy the moment. He had always been happy to stay in the shadows, but lately, he was starting to feel an overwhelming sense of loneliness. He was really enjoying being in the band and starting to get some recognition but at the same time, he longed to blend into the background and not stand out so much. Vince noticed his unease and walked over, putting his arm around him and urging him to join in the fun.

"I'm ok mate honesty," Billy shouted, trying to make himself heard above the music, "I'm just thinking about the gig, it's two nights away and I really don't want to fuck up."

"Don't worry about it," assured Vince, "It's just another show, we're going to be great." Billy nodded and took a deep breath; he knew his friend was right. He was starting to feel the excitement for the show building and he couldn't wait to perform.

The next two days passed in a blur of preparation and anticipation. On the day of the gig, the four of them made their way to the venue. By five o'clock, they finally made it into The Marquee and found the venue swarming with the road crew and management of the Australian band. Sarah Morton, who they had been trying to stay away from since they were going to replace her as their manager after tonight, was also there waiting for them.

"Hey guys," she shouted excitedly, waving over at them, "let me introduce you."

They got to meet Michael, the band's singer, a handsome man with mesmerising long curly locks. He thanked them for being the support band and said he was looking forward to seeing their performance.

Billy looked over to the bar area and saw Martin Kerry and Anthony Weston Davies deep in conversation. They were with two of their associates, although Billy didn't know them by name, they sat at their usual table on high bar stools just to the left of the main bar. He nodded across at Micky and said "It looks like another night of cock dodging after we've played tonight," before rolling his eyes and turning his attention back to what was going on near the stage. He saw Michael take his position on the stage with a microphone in hand and couldn't help but feel a sudden surge of inspiration course through him. He was mesmerised as the band performed their sound check and he could already tell they were destined for stardom. If they sounded this amazing now, what would they sound like once the show really got going?

As the band anxiously waited in their dressing room

before the show, Justin and Alicia peeked around the door. "We just wanted to wish you all luck," Alicia said with a smile that lit up the whole room. She gave them one final encouraging comment; "We'll catch up later," accompanied by a single wink of her emerald eye.

As their intro music played the band stepped onto the stage and hammered straight into their opening number. They looked out into the audience as they started their set. Billy felt so much pride. He had never thought that anything he did would be appreciated by so many people, but here they were, intrigued and enraptured with his band's music. The energy in the room was palpable, it was electric, and nothing compared to what it felt like being up on stage in front of such an appreciative crowd. As they played on, Billy felt the music coursing through his veins; he was lost in a world of sound and rhythm that he never wanted to leave. Every strum of his guitar felt effortless and every beat of the drums kept him grounded. And when it finally came time for their final number, he knew that this was the moment they had all been waiting for. The crowd was cheering; the energy in the room was at an all-time high. The band gave it their all and when they finally finished, the room erupted. Billy felt like he was on top of the world as they took their final bow and left the stage. Back in their dressing room, the band were in high spirits, they had played one of the best shows of their lives and they knew it.

Chapter Eleven

The band congratulated each other on their performance and were still in disbelief at the amount of adoration from the crowd. Though Billy was already planning how they would top it next time. "Fucking hell Billy," exclaimed Paul, "let's just fucking well enjoy this one first!"

As he spoke, Justin and Alicia walked through the door, much to everyone's surprise. She congratulated each one of them on their performance, each member standing a little taller as she praised them with words of admiration. "You were incredible out there!" she said with a beaming grin," before she began to explain her plans for them. They felt a surge of excitement as Alicia described her vision for the band. She spoke animatedly about her contacts in the music industry and her strategy for getting their music heard by a wider audience. She talked about recording sessions and promotional tours, and for the first time, Billy felt like they were on the cusp of something monumental happening. Justin nodded along, occasionally interjecting with his own ideas and suggestions. The rest of the band listened intently, hardly daring to believe that all of this was really happening to them. They couldn't thank Justin and Alicia enough for their support and promised to work hard to make sure they lived up to their potential. A meeting was arranged for later that week to formalise everything.

Justin glanced behind him as he reached into his jacket and pulled out a small, clear pouch with white powder inside. "So," he said with a mischievous smile, "who's up for a toot?" Vince immediately responded with an enthusiastic "Yes!" and was followed by the rest of the band.

"This is just a one-time special occasion," Alicia insisted. "And since I'm the only lady here, I think it's my turn first."

After Alicia had snorted a line of the powder from the mirror she'd taken from her handbag, everyone else followed her lead and took some as well. Micky reached for the cooler box in the corner of the room and grabbed bottles to celebrate their good news and each other's company. Suddenly, the first chords from the headline band rang out, indicating that they had started their set. Excitedly, they all rushed out to enjoy the show.

Billy listened to the first couple of songs from the

side of the stage but the intense atmosphere, combined with all the alcohol and drugs he'd taken made him crave more. He forced himself through the glass exits at the back of the room, which led into the bar area where it was a bit calmer, yet he could still see through the transparent walls that were supported by three brick pillars. He moved to the bar and was about to order when he felt someone behind him.

A heavy, musky odour filled the air, the smell of cigar smoke mingling with gin and sweat. The raspy breathing echoed in his ear as he felt something hard press against his buttocks through his leather trousers. He felt a hand grope at his crotch, before sliding up to grip his backside and pull him tighter against the man behind him.

"Hey pretty boy," said the voice of Antony Weston Davies. "Are you going to let me buy you a drink? "

Billy was taken aback by the sudden proposition and tried to pull away, but the grip only tightened. He felt a surge of anger rise in his chest and quickly spun around, pushing Weston Davies back but he was too big and heavy and he found himself trapped against the bar."

"Fuck off Antony, I don't want anything from you," hissed Billy full of drink and drugs.

The sickly sweet scent of his cologne mixed with the heavy smell of alcohol and sweat was enough to make him feel nauseous. Antony Weston Davies just stared at Billy, a twisted grin slowly forming on his lips. "You know, you'd be better off inside with your friends," he said nodding his head towards the main room, "You wouldn't want to miss out on the music now would you? Although it might be worth taking a chance and seeing what else might happen tonight."

Billy was a jumble of conflicting emotions, fear mixed with anger, yet unable to gain control of any of them.

"Fuck you," he spat, "Fuck off back to your cronies and leave me alone."

Before he could get any further, Billy felt a hand on his shoulder and turned to see Vince standing behind him.

"Hey mate," Vince whispered in his ear, "settle down and come with me, there's people who want to talk to you."

The anger he'd felt dissipated slightly and he focused on what Vince was saying.

"Come on, let's go join the party," Vince said and he grabbed hold of Billy's arm and pulled him away from Weston Davies. The two of them walked away without another word to the man who stood behind them, still watching with a sly smirk on his face.

Billy looked back one last time and saw Weston Davies raise his glass at them in mock salute.

Once they had left the bar, Billy let out a sigh of relief when he realised how he had reacted and the fact that it was Vince who had saved him from a potentially volatile situation.

As they passed through the crowd, he stopped and turned to Vince and apologised for his outburst. "Sorry about that back there," he said softly, his voice filled with shame at what had happened.

Vince just smiled and nodded, squeezing Billy's shoulder gently in reassurance.

"Don't worry about it mate," Vince replied calmly, "Come on, let's go have some fun!"

Billy looked up at the stage and quickly became engrossed in the band, they were creating an energy he hadn't felt before, and they really were good. As he stood there, nodding his head and enjoying it, two girls appeared and stood either side of him.

"Your band was great tonight," a blond with blue streaks in her hair shouted in his ear trying to be heard above the music.

"Thanks," shouted back Billy and he turned back to the stage to watch.

After three encores the Australian band finally left the stage and the lights came on, illuminating the main room. The crowd began to filter out and the blond girl smiled and then took a step closer before she said, "You know if you wanted, we could all go back to our place for some drinks. What do you say?" Billy was desperate to get away from The Marquee tonight given his altercation earlier and he quickly nodded his head in agreement. Smiling back at the girls he said "Sure why not! That sounds like fun!"

The two girls clapped happily, and then linked arms with Billy and they headed out into the night air. The girls' flat was just a few streets away so they set off walking through the dark alleys filled with anticipation for what lay ahead. Soon they reached an old building with a rusty fire escape leading up to one of the upper floors. One of the girls pulled out her keys and unlocked the door on the ground floor. As they stepped through into an open hallway, then through the girl's front door, Billy quickly noticed how beautiful this place was. Streetlight filtered in through large windows, which were covered by thick velvet curtains that hung elegantly to either side. Softly coloured rugs added warmth to cold wooden floors while metallic lamps glowed dimly in each corner of the room offering just enough light to make each detail visible, there were candles burning on every available surface filling it with an inviting atmosphere, bookshelves filled with music magazines, cassette tapes and old vinyl records. Framed photographs hung high around zany art prints.

The girls led him further into one of the bedrooms where music was already playing, filling the room with an intoxicating beat. They all sat down on the bed, and the girls offered Billy a drink. As they drank and chatted, their hands began to touch him in a way that made him feel wanted and desired.

Three hours later Billy found himself out on the street, the light rain had started again and early morning was fast approaching. He looked up at the sky and it was slowly beginning to brighten. He smiled to himself as he replayed the last few hours. Vince had been right, enjoying himself and having some fun had worked wonders to relieve him of his bad mood. He walked alone along the streets of Soho. A slight mist lingered in the air, he thought about the show last night as he walked slowly, savouring every second until it cleared. The air was getting colder and he turned up his jacket collar against the chill. As he walked, he noticed how much calmer London was in the morning compared to its lively hustle and bustle during the day. He looked around taking in every detail, noticing everything from the patterned street signs to intricate graffiti on brick walls. He eventually made his way to the river Thames, feeling it's cold embrace as he stood along its banks taking in the view. The sun was starting to rise and paint London a beautiful orange hue, the sky looked like a watercolour painting. The tall buildings glowed against the turquoise sky as if they were ornaments hung in celebration of the morning. A gentle breeze blew in from the east, carrying with it the faint smell of sea salt. As he looked out over the river, people began to appear, dog walkers, runners and cyclists all making their way out for their morning routines. Billy smiled at how peaceful this moment was, a moment away from his worries and everyday life, a moment that felt almost magical. He watched as small boats cut through the glassy surface of the Thames like ghosts moving silently in an unknown direction. He took it all in with wide eyes, his heart filled with joy at this simple pleasure that life had bestowed upon him. With one last glance he turned away from the river Thames and strode confidently back towards the town eager to explore whatever lay ahead for him. He eventually made his way to Trafalgar Square where the sun was now fully visible in the sky, the tall majestic lions standing guard around Nelson's Column, Trafalgar Square fountain with its sparkling water and bright mosaic tiling. He noticed a lot of people gathered around the square, locals out for their morning walks, it felt alive, vibrant and welcoming despite its imposing grandeur.

He decided he needed something to keep him going so he set off towards one of the small cafes tucked away in a side street just off the square. The smell of freshly brewed coffee filled his senses as it beckoned him in from the street. Inside was warm and inviting with cosy booths near large windows offering plenty of natural light. He ordered a breakfast sandwich with coffee before settling down at one of the tables to enjoy his meal whilst people watching through the windowpanes. The chatter around him hummed in all languages from French to Japanese but most were speaking English, there was an unmistakable energy about this place, Billy felt at peace, it was the perfect place for him to gather his thoughts and prepare himself before heading back to Muswell Hill and the Queens Hotel.

Chapter Twelve

Billy stepped down from the iconic, double-decker London bus and made his way along Queens Avenue to the hotel. He stopped outside to take in its rundown features and the peeling paint on the walls, it had seen better days he thought as he walked up the steps and inside. The lobby was small but very tired with dried leaves scattered around in corners and furniture that had seen plenty of wear. The receptionist, a middle aged man with greasy hair greeted him warmly and handed him a key to his room. He walked slowly along the corridor and took a deep breath as he put the key in the door, the slightly musty smell teasing his nostrils. Once inside he looked around the room and smiled, he quickly realised that Micky and Vince had brought girls back last night and they'd had a bit of a party!

Clothes littered the floor, pillows were carelessly scattered across the beds, and beer cans were spilled over the furniture. Empty vodka bottles lay abandoned on the carpet. As he surveyed the room, he noticed Vince lying in bed between two girls both snoring away in blissful light sleep. He lifted his head slightly and winked at him. Billy smiled back and shook his head. His smile vanished as he looked across to the other side of the room. The lump in the bed, his bed, was covered by tangled sheets, but he could make out two sets of arms and two sets of legs splayed across the mattress. He could see a black mass of curly hair like a patch of spilled ink and he assumed that Micky lay there somewhere with a girl he'd brought back from the gig last night. Billy wished Vince good morning before slowly turning and heading back out into the hallway.

He leaned back against the wall and let out a deep sigh. It was one thing to have a good time, but he couldn't help but feel a sense of emptiness in the aftermath. He had been searching for something; he just didn't quite know what it was. As he stood there lost in thought, he heard a door creak open. It was Micky, looking even worse for wear than Vince. He stumbled past him, murmuring something about needing a shower.

With nothing left to do, he decided to explore the city. As he walked, he found himself wandering aimlessly through streets and alleyways. He passed by small markets and stopped at a bakery to pick up a coffee and something to eat. The smell of warm, crusty bread filled his senses as he savoured the aroma. He strolled on through the streets, he noticed people hurrying to and fro, cars honking as they navigated through the traffic. It was all so fast-paced, so overwhelming, so far from the peace he'd felt earlier at the cafe in Trafalgar Square. Billy found no comfort here, no sense of belonging in this chaotic city.

As he walked, he came across a small park tucked away at the end of a quiet street. It was a tranquil place, with a small pond in the centre and a few benches scattered around the outskirts. He settled himself on a bench, the takeaway coffee cup warm in his hand, and took in the peaceful surroundings.

"It's time I found myself a place of my own," he said to himself as he got up and made his way out of the park searching for somewhere to buy a newspaper.

He stumbled upon a local estate agency that caught his eye due to its yellow signboard and bright window display. There was a number of rental properties but all way out of his price range. Billy narrowed his search down to one place in particular that caught his eye. It was a small flat south of the river, one bedroom, but it would be perfect. He made an appointment to go view it in person later that day and as he walked out onto the street again, he exhaled deeply feeling hopeful about this new chapter in his life.

The only thing preventing him from moving forward was money; he knew that if he felt the flat was right for him he'd need a deposit. On the corner of the street, he noticed a line of bright red telephone boxes and rushed towards them. Fumbling in his pockets, searching for some coins, he dialled a familiar number. His mum, Pauline answered in her happy, cheerful voice.

"Hi," he said quickly, trying to sound upbeat.

"Billy," she sang into the receiver, "I was just thinking about you, is everything ok? Are you alright?"

He took a deep breath and faltered. "I think I've found the flat I want to rent, mum, it's perfect but I need a deposit and I'm not sure how I'm going to manage that. Can you lend me the money? Please?"

Seeing that she had been expecting this call for some time now, Pauline instantly agreed to lend him the money.

Billy let out a sigh of relief and promised to pay her back as soon as he could. He hung up and stood there for a moment, feeling grateful for his mum's support once again. Whenever he needed someone, she was always there.

Exiting Clapham North tube station, Billy stepped out into the cold November sunshine. He strolled down the high road before turning right onto Edgeley Road. After walking for approximately five hundred yards, he had reached his new place of residence, a one bedroom flat on the first floor of a three-story terrace house. Slipping his key into the front door, Billy entered his home.

The flat was small, but it had everything he needed, a

living room with a tiny kitchen, a bathroom and a bedroom. It was perfect.

There was a payphone in the hallway and Billy called the hotel to speak to Vince,

"What time are we meeting for rehearsals mate?" he asked when Vince picked up the receiver.

"Paul and Micky are getting there about two o'clock but I'll be a bit later. I'm going to see about somewhere to live then I'll get over there as soon as I can."

"Perfect," replied Billy, "we can get on with getting everything tight until you get there. Are we still meeting with Alicia later to sign the contracts?"

"Yes mate, her and Justin are meeting us about seven, I think the idea is to sign and then get some dates sorted out for the recording."

"That's great news, good luck with the house hunting, I'll see you later."

Billy placed the receiver back on the phone and raced upstairs to get his things together, he grabbed his guitar and rushed back out of the flat. With a newfound burst of energy, he ran back to Clapham North tube station.

Micky, Paul and Billy spent the afternoon going through their set, tightening things up and working on their harmonies, looking forward to finally getting in the recording studio with a top producer. Vince hadn't made it, but they assumed he would meet them later.

At seven o'clock, Alicia and Justin arrived at the

hotel lobby where they'd agreed to meet. Billy could feel his heart rate spike, as he was about to sign the contract that could soon see his music dreams come true. He noticed Alicia was wearing a vintage black dress with silver stitching around the edges and a deep purple velvet blazer. She had her hair swept up and looked absolutely amazing.

Justin on the other hand had quite a different vibe about him appearing much more serious than Alicia, dressed smartly in an all-black suit with an open neck shirt and aviator sunglasses tucked into his pocket.

Vince had managed to get there about ten minutes earlier having spent the afternoon organising a place for himself to live. Billy, Micky, Paul and Vince all signed their contracts without hesitation, excitement coursing through their veins at what this could mean for them as performers and artists. They discussed upcoming recording dates and plans for the future. Justin explained that he'd like to get in the studio next week and record two songs to begin with; he suggested Someday Remember and Still Forever, as those were two of the songs that he'd been most impressed with at The Marquee gig. Arrangements were made for them to be at East/West studios in Acton the following Monday but before then Alicia explained that she needed some promotion photos to begin her campaign with.

The following day, the band arrived at a photo studio in Victoria. When they got there, it immediately felt special, the studio was huge with hardwood floors and white walls that gave off such a perfect contrast against the Stellar silver backdrop. An old whirring fan oscillated gently in one corner of the room filling it with a warmth that made everyone feel comfortable.

The photographer, a camp Frenchman called Pierre, started to get to work setting up his camera while Alicia organised her team which included two assistants carrying boxes full of clothes and general props to use during the shoot. As she bustled around making sure everything was ready, Billy couldn't help but think about how much talent and passion she brought to everything she did. She seemed like an expert in her field and he wondered how far she could take them.

Once Pierre had set up, he called out for everyone to take his or her places. The band geared up with their instruments and took their spots on a stage like area that had been set up with lights surrounding them while Alicia positioned herself behind Pierre giving instructions as he clicked away taking photos from different angles capturing them perfectly. As they started having fun some really amazing shots were taken which Alicia promised she would show them in due course. After around four hours of shooting Pierre eventually declared himself happy with all of the images he'd captured. As they packed up he told Alicia that he'd get something back to her to look at within a week.

The day had been long and tiring but it was the

beginning of something special. They all went their separate ways, a feeling of excitement bubbling inside them all for what tomorrow might bring.

Billy sat on the worn sofa in his flat, it had been a great day and although he was tired, he wasn't ready for bed. He decided he'd get himself ready and take a walk round the local area to see if anything was happening anywhere.

As he got ready, he couldn't help but feel a sense of liberation. He had his own place now, his music career was finally taking off, and he was free to explore the world around him. He quickly slipped on his leather jacket, feeling the coolness of the material against his skin as he stepped out into the chilly November night.

The high road was alive with people, couples hand in hand; groups of friends laughing and chatting away, and the thumping sound of music could be heard coming from a nearby bar. Billy smiled to himself as he walked past, feeling a sudden urge to go in and have a drink.

The bar was busy; the atmosphere was thick with the scent of alcohol and cigarette smoke. Billy squeezed his way to the bar and ordered himself a beer, taking a seat on a stool. As he sipped his drink, he watched the people around him, lost in their own worlds.

As he sat there, drinking, smoking and enjoying the loud music, he found himself thinking about Alicia, the way she moved and spoke with such confidence and passion. He couldn't help but feel drawn to her, wanting to know more about her as a person. He shook his head, trying to snap out of it. He had to focus on his music, his career, and making a name for himself. Relationships should be the last thing on his mind. Plus, she was a lot older than him and married to Justin. He bought himself another drink and put the thought to the back of his mind.

Chapter Thirteen

The following week seemed like a long one for the band. The four of them were eager to see what Pierre had been able to capture during their photo shoot. As the weekend drew closer, there was an air of excitement as they waited for news that they'd be able to go over and see the final results.

During rehearsals Vince went out to the reception area and took a call from Alicia, she told him to bring everyone down to the office as soon as they'd finished for the day. Three hours later they were on the tube to Sloane Square, eager to see the photos of themselves.

As soon as they arrived, Alicia eagerly took out the folder containing all of the images from the shoot. Everyone leaned forward in anticipation as she began passing round photos revealing amazing shots of each individual member along with some stunning group images that looked like they belonged on a magazine cover.

Each one of them looked on in amazement at how good they looked, captured at their best angles and lit by fantastic lighting against stunning backgrounds. They were overwhelmed by it all and acknowledged that finding such a talent like Pierre had definitely been worth the wait!

They were in high spirits after seeing the photo shoot results and decided to go out and celebrate. Everyone piled out of the office and made their way to a little place they liked just off the Kings Road. Micky quickly grabbed a round of drinks whilst Vince hunted for an empty table. They settled down in a corner of the bar for what promised to be an enjoyable night ahead!

The night turned out to be a bit of a wild one. Billy and the band had a great time drinking and laughing as they looked forward to their upcoming recording session. They were all enjoying themselves so much that they lost track of time and before they knew it, it was already past midnight.

As the bar closed and they said their goodbyes, Alicia reminded them that they were about to begin a recording session with one of the best producers around and that they should make sure to take advantage of it. They thanked her for giving them the opportunity and promised to make it worthwhile. After making his way home, Billy was full of energy and excitement at the thought of getting into the studio again. He picked up his guitar and played through the songs they were going to record. He couldn't wait for what promised to be an unforgettable experience!

The following Monday, they arrived at the East/West studios bright and early, ready to begin their session. As soon as they walked in, it was clear that this wasn't going to be like any other studio session they'd been involved in. Everywhere they looked, they saw state of the art equipment that promised a unique sound unlike anything they'd had before.

Justin was already there waiting, he greeted them warmly and introduced his sound engineer Jon Marshall.

He had very particular ideas behind the session and made sure to explain everything he expected from them as they went along. On the first day, they spent most of their time getting the right sounds. Micky arranged his drums on a riser at the back and microphones were placed around each drum. Two were placed directly above him and two more out in front to create a full sound. Billy and Paul stayed behind sound screens to cut down on overspill, while Vince was isolated in a vocal booth that prompted much teasing from the other three who had the pleasure of being together in the live room. After three days of hard work, everyone crowded into the control room to listen to their track, Someday Remember, and it sounded like a hit.

"Fucking hell," yelled Micky. "Is that really us?"

"You better believe it," said Justin, beaming with pride. "I'm really pleased with this one. I'm going to take a mix home and have another listen in a few days, then we'll come back for our final mix."

"Final mix?" Vince asked amazed at how great it already sounded.

"Yeah," Justin explained. "I want to hear it with fresh ears. There's always something I can find to improve once I've taken some time away from it."

Everyone understood that it was a good idea to have time away from the recording for a while and the band thanked Justin for his efforts before packing up their equipment and joining their roadies Jimmy and Fang outside, Vince wanting to reward them for their hard work over the last couple of months by buying them a drink or two. After three hard days in the studio, they didn't look their best and decided not to visit any of their usual places. Instead, Jimmy recommended The Black Flag, an old school pub situated on the corner of New Cross Road and James Street; it was down in South East London near the railway tracks. From the outside it looked similar to the one of the bars Billy had seen in an old-fashioned gangster film he'd watched a few weeks ago. Sure enough, when they stepped in through the entrance he knew he'd been right.

Jimmy was already known around the pub, it seemed that there wasn't anyone who didn't recognise him. He had a wry smile on his face as he led them to a back room. He was in his early thirties. He had shoulder length sandy hair and a long droopy moustache, his skin was pale and he had dark brown eyes, he was only around five foot five but he was solidly built and he could look after himself. His laugh resounded through the room and lit up his whole face. It became immediately clear why Vince trusted him with their gear, not only did he know exactly how to take care of it, but people just warmed to him instantly, mainly due to his charisma.

Fang on the other hand looked as if he'd been born in this place, as if he'd been living off the stories people told here. He was calm, almost thoughtful, which belied the mischievous look in his eyes. He had short-cropped hair and piercings in both ears, his nose and upper lip. When he smiled he revealed a gap where he was missing his two front teeth. He had a knack for making you feel completely at ease whilst listening intently to every word you said. They were both the sort of characters you wanted on your side. As Paul went over to order more drinks, it was evident that apart from being incredibly loyal and resourceful, Jimmy also had an impressive network of contacts around East London, especially amongst the regulars in shady places like The Black Flag.

Billy decided that he wouldn't drink excessively this evening and remain in control. One careless word amongst this type of crowd could land him in a lot of trouble.

Jimmy was a natural storyteller and as the night went

on, he began to tell them stories of his childhood growing up in East London. He'd always been a bit of an adventurer, looking for excitement wherever he could find it. He began to share some of his experiences in the shady parts of East London. He had seen it all, gambling dens, thugs, drug dealers and spoke as if he were a part of it all. Fang on the other hand, was a bit of an enigma. He never seemed to want to talk about himself or what he did on nights like this, he preferred to smile knowingly and listen intently. This lack of participation only added to the air of mystery that surrounded him. The conversation switched to some of the characters they had been warned about, with stories of gambling and brawls and as the night wore on, more people began to enter the pub. The atmosphere began to shift. It was almost like a gathering of local villains but Jimmy seemed surprisingly relaxed in this situation and even made a few jokey remarks now and then which caused some nervous chuckles amongst the group. Everything seemed a little different in this place, even their drinks seemed never ending, it was as if no matter what round they ordered, they never ran out.

At two in the morning, Jimmy led the group out onto New Cross Road, all of them eager for the journey home. At the mini cab office opposite the pub, Billy, Paul and Micky got into one car while Vince and Fang shared another. They had made a plan to meet up again on Saturday night, but as Billy sat in the back of the cab, he couldn't help but feel uneasy. Something about the night had unnerved him. He couldn't quite put his finger on it, but the shady atmosphere of the pub and the presence of the local villains had left him feeling on edge. As they pulled up outside his flat, he quickly handed Paul some cash and got out, eager to be alone.

But as he lay in his bed, thoughts of the recording session and the night at The Black Flag still swirling in his head, a sense of excitement began to build. He knew that this was only the beginning for him and the band. If they could create something as great as Someday Remember in just three days, who knew what they could accomplish in the future? He was keen to see where this journey would take him. And with the support of his band mates and the guidance of Justin and Alicia, he was ready to face whatever challenges lay ahead.

Chapter Fourteen

Billy rolled out of bed at 10am, his stomach rumbling with hunger. The studio sessions had been going on late every night and they had only stopped for a fast food delivery or a quick trip to the pizza place opposite. He searched the cupboards in the kitchen, where he found tea, sugar, beans, and a tin of tuna. The fridge was equally unhelpful with its six-day old milk, one egg, and a half tub of margarine. He put on some jeans and rummaged through the pockets searching for cash, finding a five-pound note and some coins. Wearing an old jumper and trainers, not particularly stylish he thought but he really didn't care, he grabbed his jacket and ran out to 'The Hole In The Wall', a makeshift eatery serving food from a side window of an end terrace near the tube station. He hurried back home with a sausage and egg roll that tasted as if it had been made by the angels. The day was off to a perfect start!

Having finished his breakfast, he made himself a cup of tea and sank into his cosy worn cream sofa with a sigh. Everything had been so chaotic lately; he needed time for himself to relax and now seemed like the perfect opportunity to enjoy some peace and solitude. As he sipped his tea, he began thinking about his life and the journey he'd been on so far but the band was only just getting started and he knew that there were more hurdles to overcome.

He decided to spend the rest of the day practising, using the time to work on some of the new songs they'd been writing. Music was his escape and he knew he would never tire of it.

When evening arrived, he thought about going out for a quiet drink on his own. He put down his guitar and grabbed his keys, deciding to take a walk. He had been so caught up in studio sessions and rehearsals, that he hadn't had much opportunity to explore the area. He'd had enough of pubs and clubs, but the thought of having a quiet drink on his own felt comforting and calming. He took a deep breath of the cool evening air and started walking, not really sure where he was heading but he finally made it to the White Swan, an imposing place at the end of the high road up by the common. He stepped into the pub and strode up to the bar where he ordered himself a pint of lager. Noticing an empty table in the window, he walked over to it and settled down to enjoy his drink. He lit a cigarette and smiled to himself as he thought about all the great things going on in his life.

He sipped at his pint, relishing the cool, crisp taste, dreams of stardom and success revolving around his head. What would it all look like? He wasn't quite sure. Being anonymous and able to do what he liked without being noticed appealed to him, being recognised every time he went out would surely change the balance he had in his life just now. What did he really want? Maybe he was jumping too far ahead he thought to himself, just take one step at a time. When he'd finished his drink he decided to head off. Although it was tempting to get another one, he decided against it and made himself a cup of tea when he got home. He kicked off his boots, and settled down on the sofa to watch a film, looking forward to having another day to himself tomorrow before catching up with his friends on Saturday to begin a new chapter in The Innocent's story.

On Saturday morning Billy walked up to the bank on the high road to check his balance, he hadn't used all the money his mum had sent him for the deposit and was pleasantly surprised to find he had enough money to get himself some food for the week and still have enough for a good night out later. He withdrew £20 and walked over to the supermarket opposite. He grabbed a trolley from a long line of them outside and wandered amongst the aisles picking out things he really fancied. Twenty minutes later, armed with three bags of food, forty cigarettes and a bottle of vodka he made his way back to his flat and started unpacking, when he'd put everything away, his fridge, cupboards and freezer looked healthier than they ever had done.

The afternoon was spent noodling on his guitar whilst watching an old black and white film and enjoying an occasional sip of vodka and coke.

Around five o'clock, after watching the full time football results he decided it was time to get ready to go out. They'd all agreed to meet in the 100 Club on Oxford Street at nine o'clock but he was going to go out a bit earlier and see what else was going on.

He peeled himself off the sofa and made his way to the shower before drying himself off and stepping back into his bedroom. He dressed in his customary tight jeans and cowboy boots, black vest and black shirt with a red rose pattern. He spent a good ten minutes sorting his hair out, then he applied some black eyeliner and grabbed his favourite black leather jacket, he picked up his keys and strode confidently out of his front door for what promised to be a thrilling evening.

He made his way to the tube station and jumped onto a train heading into town. The carriage filled with people, the secretive conversations, fleeting glances and barely suppressed laughter made Billy smile inside as the stations sped by. When he arrived at Oxford Circus he hopped off eager to see what wonders were waiting for him. He walked down Regent Street, past Piccadilly

Circus and its bright lights, and then turned left into Soho.

He wandered around admiring the sights, portraits of unknown stars on old theatre walls, Italian restaurants that promised more than just a good dinner, speakers blasting out music from open doors across brightly lit clubs. Every twist and turn he took revealed something new to investigate and enjoy until eventually he made it to Dean Street and the jazz club he'd been meaning to get to for ages, he stepped inside through the neon lit doorway and headed downstairs. He didn't particularly like jazz, it was his dad and his uncle James who had really enjoyed it and they'd played for hours on end in a jazz trio. Despite his reservations about the music, he really did appreciate the amazing ability of the individual musicians; it was just that he could only ever think of it as musical wanking, to him it sounded like everyone was playing random pieces of music at the same time. The thing he really enjoyed about jazz clubs was the sleazy, smoky atmosphere and laid back ambience. He bought himself a drink at the bar and sat alone at a table near the stage. It was early, and the club hadn't really filled up yet. Billy surveyed the scene, watching as a male pianist in his sixties and a girl in her late teens played their rendition of Fly Me To The Moon. It wasn't exactly what he was looking for, so Billy gulped down his drink and left to search for another place.

As he left the jazz club he walked straight into Nigel,

the bass player in a band that was getting a fair amount of recognition and someone that Billy had struck up a friendship with. Nigel said he was on his way to The Bath House, a traditional pub on the corner of Dean Street and Shaftesbury Avenue popular with musicians, and he invited him to tag along. He was more than happy to join him and the two strode off together.

As soon as they were inside, Nigel manoeuvred his way to the bar and ordered the drinks. It was packed inside but they found a space near the stairs and began talking about recording music and the tour that Nigel's band was about to embark on. Billy was having a great time until he realised that they'd almost finished their drinks and he made his way to the bar for another round. As he struggled to grab the barman's attention, a woman with jet-black hair sidled up next to him. She said something too quietly for him to make out, but he smiled back at her anyway. She stepped nearer and shouted over the noise of the bar, "I heard your band was amazing at The Marquee the other night!"

"Thanks very much!" Billy responded. "Were you there?"

"No, I had to work, but my friends told me how good you were!"

"Thank you, I really appreciate that," Billy replied, a bit embarrassed. "I'm going to take these drinks back. Maybe I'll see you again later?"

"Maybe," she said with a flirtatious wink.

He walked back over to Nigel and the two of them continued their chat until Nigel said he had to go meet his girlfriend as he was buying her dinner. Billy said he hoped to meet again soon and wished him luck on the tour.

He headed to the toilets then decided to get himself another drink while he thought of somewhere else to go. On his way to the bar he ran into the black haired woman again, who was now with a friend, an older woman with bleached blond hair scraped up in a pony-tail that accentuated her harsh features.

"Has your mate gone now?" she asked as he squeezed past.

"Yeah, gone to meet his girlfriend, can I get you a drink?" he asked, surprised at himself for offering.

"No thanks, we've just got one. Thanks for the offer though."

He bought himself another drink then went back and stood near the two women. The one with the black hair, who Billy quite liked the look of, introduced herself as Kelly and her friend was called Monica. They chatted for a while and Billy discovered that Kelly worked part time in a hostess bar just off Berwick Street, Monica didn't say what she did but he suspected it was the same sort of thing, she had a look about her. He could sense that something wasn't quite right but he was enjoying himself so he didn't give it too much thought. They chatted and drank for another hour or so then Billy announced he was going to meet his band in the 100 Club.

"We'll walk up with you," said Kelly, "see who's around."

As they left the pub and began to walk along Dean Street, Billy told them that he needed to get some more cash. He walked over to the bank on the corner of Richmond Mews and put his bankcard into the cash machine. He punched in his four digit PIN number then a powerful blow to the back of his head pushed him forward, smashing his nose against the cold metal frame of the ATM. As he tried to work out what had happened he felt another blow just below his kidneys leaving him winded and in agony. He was knocked to the floor and a kick connected with the side of his head. More kicks rained down on him, more blows pounded the back of his head until finally, he looked up to see a hard, spiteful face staring down at him, a sick smirk spreading across her lips. Kelly was at the machine but before Billy could process what had happened, both women had vanished, leaving him lying in a broken heap in the street as the rain began to pour down. He lay on the hard, wet concrete for a moment, trying to comprehend what had happened. He could feel warm liquid around his legs as he slowly realised that he had both pissed and shat himself in the attack. He lay there, feeling utterly humiliated and scared but knowing that he somehow had to get up, he saw that his bankcard was still in the machine although he suspected his account was now empty. He could taste a sharp, metallic tang in his mouth; he pulled his hand away from his head finding blood on his fingertips. He pulled himself up and slowly stumbled away. Tears mixed with raindrops on his cheeks as waves of nausea choked inside him.

He made his way to Vauxhall Bridge aware of the stares of passers by but too ashamed to even look up. He felt stupid and violated but knew that the real shame was knowing how easily he'd been fooled. When he finally made it home, he staggered inside, sinking to his knees in despair. The stench that clung to him was overwhelming. He stripped off his filthy clothes and tossed them into the bathtub running hot water over them in a desperate attempt to remove the humiliation. He stood underneath the steaming hot water of the shower for what seemed like an eternity, how could he ever show his face outside again?

CHAPTER FIFTEEN

Billy became increasingly paranoid and anxious anytime he left his house. He still had to meet with Vince and the band for rehearsals and all the other things that were going on, to keep things moving forward as best he could. He was drinking heavily, all the once familiar streets now filled him with dread and foreboding, sending chills down his spine every time he walked past the scene of his humiliation. He would make excuses to leave band meetings early and try and avoid the nights out blaming some sort of virus or any other ailment he could think of. Every time he stepped out of his front door, paranoia crept in, making him feel vulnerable and exposed. He began to avoid going into town and Soho in particular as much as possible, jumping at any sudden noise or movement. Dark alleyways sickened him and crowded streets gave him an overwhelming feeling of terror. He kept glancing over his shoulder for Kelly and

Monica or anyone else who might want to do him harm, but really he knew that it was foolish, he told himself that they wouldn't be anywhere, deep down he knew it was safe, but the nagging doubts persisted. At home, Billy slept badly, startled awake by the slightest sound while nightmares ran rampant through his mind making it difficult for him to rest for long periods at a time. During the day, he stayed indoors languishing under this self-imposed exile with only his thoughts to keep him company and stave off loneliness but they usually did little more than bring back painful memories from that fateful night on Dean Street.

At least he still had his music to hold onto, he spent more and more time in rehearsals, he would stay behind after the others had left, finding a solace attacking his guitar with an intensity he'd never felt before. He immersed himself in the music, playing every song with such ferocity that it was almost as if he was punishing himself for being attacked. His playing became increasingly frenzied as if by playing harder and faster he could expunge the past memories from his mind. He would come to rehearsal exhausted and drained, having barely slept during the night. No one but Billy knew what happened that night, or what brought on this new intensity of his playing. It seemed that no matter how hard he played or how loud the music got, he could never seem to drown out the memory of Monica's malicious smirk forever embedded in his mind.

The months went by and slowly, Billy began to take back control of his life, using music as an outlet for the pain and hurt that still lingered inside. He slowly started going out again; happy to meet with Alicia to discuss the next steps for the band, conquering each fear one step at a time. He'd meet Vince and the others for a night out and when he left them, he'd walk around Soho late at night when the streets were quiet, steeling himself against any potential danger or triggers from the night of the attack. As time went by, he gradually gained back some of the confidence he had lost and found solace in the familiar rhythms and melodies that allowed him to express his innermost emotions in ways words never could. The healing process was slow but steady as Billy gradually regained control over his life and moved forward, knowing that it was possible to move past the horrors of his attack.

One evening, just as he'd walked through the front door of his house the phone in the hallway began ringing. As he answered it, he heard Alicia's voice on the other end informing him that Justin and the rest of the band would be at Air Recording Studios in Hampstead at 11 o'clock the following morning to remix Someday Remember. It had been about six months since they'd first recorded with Justin but he'd been called away to work in America and this was the first opportunity he'd had to get back in the studio to finish what they'd started. Billy was thrilled, it was just the news he needed, he was getting some of his confidence back and being able to finish the recording and get a release date for their first single was the perfect tonic.

"Thanks Alicia, that's great news, I'll be there at 11," he said excitedly into the receiver, "will you be there too?"

"No, I've got a busy day tomorrow," she replied "I'm meeting a film director to discuss a date for you guys to film a video. I want to get a great package together seeing as it's our first release."

"Wow that's amazing," gushed Billy, "it's been really quiet for months and now everything's going crazy again, I can't wait!"

"Well I'm doing all I can," continued Alicia, "you get over to the studio in the morning then hopefully we'll all get together later in the week to put some solid plans in place."

Billy promised to be there and they said their goodbyes.

The next day, Billy arrived at the studio early, the rest of the band arrived at the same time, not wanting to miss anything that Justin had planned for the remix of Someday Remember. When they got inside, they were amazed at what Justin had come up with. He had taken the songs they'd recorded months ago and transformed them into something truly unique and exciting. As they worked through each mix, Justin explained everything to them in great detail so that everyone understood exactly what was going on and gave their input into how each section should sound. Together, they worked on perfecting the final intricacies of the two songs in order to get them exactly how they wanted for the release. They worked late into the night until finally it was time to call it a night and go home.

As Billy sat on the tube home, he felt an intense sense of pride and accomplishment rushing through his veins, something he hadn't felt since before his attack six months prior. He didn't think that this could be possible, but here he was heading home after spending a few hours working in one of London's most prestigious studios alongside one of the best producers in the country and probably the best sound engineer around. The future suddenly seemed full of exciting possibilities, plans had begun to form about when Someday Remember would be released and what the music video would look like, everything seemed amazing!

Billy looked forward to reuniting with Alicia and the band later in the week when she'd have news about the video for their first single. It seemed that nothing could stop them now.

Later that week, Alicia called them all to a meeting at her office to tell them about the film director they were to work with. His name was Chris and, according to Alicia, Chris had worked on some of the biggest music videos of the year and had received critical acclaim for his work. His credits were too long to list but what Alicia knew for sure was that he shared their passion for music and wanted to create something special for Someday Remember's music video.

He said he was excited about the challenge of creating something that would resonate with viewers on a whole new level and as such, wanted to find out more about the band and what direction they were aiming for visually before beginning any work on set. Alicia proposed setting up a series of meetings between him and each member individually so that they could make sure everyone's ideas were heard and incorporated into the final edit.

The entire process seemed daunting, however, everyone was determined to get everything right so that they could do Someday Remember justice when it came to its official release later in the year. All in all, they felt like this partnership had come along at just the right time, it felt like things were really starting to move forward for them!

The band were excited as they discussed ideas with Chris and talked about the visuals for the video. As they brainstormed and sketched out ideas on paper, one thing was becoming increasingly clear, everyone in the group had their own unique vision for how this video should play out. Chris took all of the band's input into account and listened to what each person had to say before gradually piecing together a concept which incorporated elements from each members' idea while also adding his own creative twist. It was safe to say that when it came to visualising this particular project, Chris knew exactly what he was doing.

After many, many hours of discussion from both Chris and the band, a concept was born. The video would feature the band playing inside an old time theatre with a backdrop designed to look like a Dickensian street scene. This created an atmosphere where it felt like you were watching a story unfold rather than just seeing four people playing instruments and singing, something they'd never thought about before!

A week later, at the crack of dawn they arrived at a film studio in Camden Lock. None of them were morning people by nature, but today was an exception. The four of them were quickly ushered through the white walled studio into the makeup room, where Alicia and two other women were rummaging through boxes of cosmetics. Paul sat down in the chair first facing a mirror surrounded with spotlights while Vince pulled out a bottle of vodka from his bag.

"Fuck off!" Micky exclaimed stretching out uncomfortably, "I've only been awake for half an hour."

"It's just to relax us," Vince said calmly, "we need to look natural and relaxed on camera. We can't afford to mess it up, considering the amount we're spending."

"Pour me a large one," Paul requested from his spot under the bright lights, "my mates back in Birmingham will really take the piss when they see me dressed up like this."

A middle-aged man with blond curly hair, sporting a huge smile and wearing a white jacket, entered through the rear door carrying a tray draped in a white cloth. He placed it down in one corner of the room and whipped away the material to reveal plates piled high with bacon, sausage and racks of toast. Micky practically dived across the room, grabbing two slices of bread and layering them with four sausages and as much bacon as he could fit between them.

"This is fantastic!" He mumbled between mouthfuls of food. "Vince, pour me something to drink, I'll need it after all this."

Vince just shook his head and poured vodka into a plastic cup.

After the rest of them had taken a somewhat more civilised approach to breakfast they made their way next door to begin work. The studio had been transformed into a scene straight out of Dickens. Heavy bookshelves lined the walls, their rickety frames aged with a light coating of dust. Cobwebs hung in between stacks of tattered novels, illuminated by old-fashioned lanterns and dull candle-light. Their instruments were all given an antique look too, giving the room a dream-like atmosphere. The four of them stood together in awe, their nerves calmed by the morning Vodka. Now they just wanted to get started.

For the next eight hours, Chris directed Billy, Vince, Paul and Micky through their choreography. As they moved around the set to the same four minutes of music, sweat glistened on their faces from exertion and after each take their makeup was retouched as required. After finally finishing, they sank into the soft chairs in the dressing room, only to be called back out five minutes later. Chris announced that they were taking the shoot outside on location. Vince sang passionately as he walked down a Camden street outside an old time London pub. Strangers stopped and lined the other side of the street to watch the spectacle unfold, wondering what was happening with the four band members dressed as street urchins. They continued filming under an old iron canal bridge, where a fire had been lit in preparation for their scene. Paul and Billy settled down next to it while Vince and two dancers, members from one of Alicia's other acts performed alongside them. In the final scene, Micky walked away with an antique lantern in hand as the song faded to its conclusion. They all paused to wonder how Chris was going to piece together such diverse footage.

Two weeks later, Alicia invited the four of them to her office. Paul guessed it was time to watch the video they had created and they scrambled onto the tube and headed down to Alicia's office. As soon as they walked in, there were four glasses of champagne set on the table in front of a large sofa, a large TV screen sat opposite. She told them to take a seat and enjoy the moment with a celebratory toast before pressing play on the video recorder.

The four of them sat silent in amazement. They watched in awe as the magic of cinematography worked its way into every frame with different camera angles creating drama throughout each scene while vintage props and costumes weaved their way into nearly every shot, resulting in a truly unique piece of art which perfectly matched the soundscape Someday Remember had cultivated over its months of production.

Chris's visionary work combined with Justin's brilliant music production had created something special, adding another level of depth to their first single. It felt as if everyone involved had found something new within themselves during this particular journey.

Chapter Sixteen

Billy jolted awake in a cold sweat, his breath shallow. He looked around wildly before coming to the realisation that he was safe in his own bed. It had been another nightmare. Although they were getting rarer, they still felt all too real and brought him back to the night of his attack. The bed covers were scattered on the floor at the foot of the bed. He let out a deep sigh and rubbed his face, trying to shake off the feeling of fear that still lingered in him. It had been nearly eight months since that night when the two women had beaten him up and robbed him, it still haunted him.

He got up from his bed and went to the kitchen to make himself some tea. As the water boiled, he leaned against the worktop trying to calm his racing thoughts. He couldn't let the fear consume him again. He had come too far to let his past traumas undo all the progress he had made. He took a sip of the tea, closed his eyes and let himself focus on the warmth in his hands. As he breathed in the steam from the mug, he let his mind wander to the future, to all the exciting things they still had to accomplish as a band. They were all meeting up again tonight to discuss the arrangements for their first tour. He couldn't wait to get out of London and a tour seemed like the perfect opportunity.

Billy stepped off the tube at Tottenham Court Road and made his way down Oxford Street to meet the others, weaving through the bustling masses of people milling around in the heat of the city.

As he walked into The Ship, he scanned the crowd for Vince and the others, but he couldn't see them. He spotted Justin in the far corner of the bar chatting with a stranger. He pushed his way through the crowd towards them.

"Billy!" Justin said cheerfully when he saw him, handing him some cash. "Get yourself a drink, we'll have another round while you're up there. This is Rico, he's coming on tour with you."

Rico greeted him warmly with a smile and a hand-shake. "Billy, at last we meet, Justin's been telling me all about you."

"Oh God," Billy laughed, "anything good or just the truth?"

"No," Justin responded seriously before breaking into a grin and thumping Billy on the back. "Don't worry, it's all good stuff. I like working with you guys, and I've given

Rico fair warning that he's got his work cut out trying to keep you all under control."

As Billy stood at the bar, waiting for someone to serve him, his gaze shifted to Rico. He had dark, leathery skin that was crisscrossed with worry lines and deep-set eyes that had seemed to peer into Billy's soul. A long moustache hung from his upper lip and high cheekbones protruded from sunken cheeks, he had long, shaggy hair streaked with grey. An earring shaped like a golden snake dangled from his right ear, catching the glimmer of a nearby lantern. Beneath an aged leather jacket, he wore a red and gold waistcoat with sparkling silver buttons. The faded jeans hugged his legs; a thick leather belt was covered in various studs and badges perfect for a biker. On his feet were faded black boots that had seen many adventures. Rico looked like he had lived life to the fullest, and time was finally beginning to take its toll.

Billy took the drinks and made his way back to the others, smiling wide. He liked Rico already. Despite his weathered appearance, he exuded a natural warmth and kindness that was inviting. Billy knew immediately that Rico would be the spirit of their tour, given both his appearance and good nature. The adventure had just begun!

He had just placed the drinks on the table when Vince, Micky and Paul arrived. He was immediately sent back to the bar for more. He ordered and paid for the drinks before he made his way back to the table, where

Rico was regaling Vince and the others with some outlandish tales of his past adventures. They were all enthralled, and as Billy slid between them he found himself caught up in Rico's stories as well. His face lit up when he spoke, his hands gesticulating wildly with every word. By the time he had finished, they were all roaring with laughter and couldn't wait to get out on the road themselves.

Justin suddenly jumped up to greet a man who'd just walked in. "Steve," he said warmly, "how are you? It's been ages since I saw you, come over and join us, I want you to meet the new band I've been working with."

Steve was introduced to them all and sat down to join them, he looked around thirty and wore a sharp brown suit, an open neck white silk shirt and highly polished shoes. Apparently he worked in the music business himself and was the son of a famous comedian who was a regular on Saturday night television.

Steve began to tell them tales of his journey in the music industry. He spoke of how he'd attended performances and showcases, met influential people, made contacts and connections, and even been able to get a demo released on a major label. The more he said, the more they hung onto his every word. Steve looked from one face to the other as he continued talking, until finally Micky cleared his throat.

"So," he asked cautiously, "what do you think it takes to really make it in this business?"

Steve grinned knowingly as if he were expecting this very question. He took a sip of his drink before launching into some of the most wondrous details about making it in the music industry that they had ever heard.

The band was intently listening to Steve, until he got up to go to the bar for more drinks. When he'd left, Justin and Rico exchanged a knowing smirk before warning the band. "He's just a rich kid who's got a reputation in the music world as a bit of a joke. Don't take anything he says too seriously," Rico chuckled. "He may be a nice guy but don't believe him! He's full of shit. But he tells a good story."

The night continued on, with the band and Rico sharing stories and laughs until the barman called last orders. As they all stumbled out of The Ship, Steve called back to Micky to pick up the tapes he'd left on the windowsill; Micky dutifully picked them up and carried them outside. He handed over the tapes to Steve, who thanked him and said his goodbyes. Then Steve flagged down a black cab and he, Justin, and Rico all got in and drove away.

Three days later Vince burst into the rehearsal studio, overflowing with excitement. "Those tapes that Micky picked up were actually the masters for a music show created by a TV company. The producers and crew were in the pub celebrating the fact they'd finished the production but because they were all having such a good time the guy in charge of the tapes didn't realise that Micky had taken them," he gushed barely stopping for breath." Justin told me that Steve had taken one look at them and realised they looked out of place on the window sill, figuring there must be something special about them. Anyway, Steve returned the tapes but apparently made some kind of arrangement that resulted in us being invited to the launch party for the show. There'll be loads of people there, celebrities included, we might even get our music video played or have a spot on their live show."

"Fucking hell," said Micky with a hint of concern, "does that mean I'm in trouble now? I've still got fines that I haven't paid from back home, If I get caught again I could really be in the shit."

"Don't worry about it," Vince assured him, "Nobody knows it was you who took them. The producers are just grateful to get them back; they were the masters so it would cost them a fortune if they had to reshoot everything. I don't think they're bothered about what happened now they have them back."

"What night is the party?" asked Paul, "Where is it?

"Next Thursday," Vince told them, "we'll find out where it is later, he did tell me but I've forgotten in all the excitement. Somewhere in Camden I think."

The band couldn't wait for the launch party, excitement bubbling through each of them like a river running rampant. They had never been to anything like it before, and they had no idea how to act or what to expect. Billy was particularly nervous. He had never been a fan of large crowds unless they were playing a show. They nervously mingled with the other guests, all of whom seemed to be celebrities and industry insiders. Billy felt out of place, but he kept a smile on his face and tried to make small talk with anyone who crossed his path.

As he and Vince were talking with Paul, they recognised a familiar voice, one with a distinctive high-pitched Birmingham accent.

"Hey waiter," it sounded, cutting through the room. "What's this stuff in the orange juice?"

"That's champagne sir," replied the waiter, "would you like some more?"

The three of them wanted the room to swallow them up but they just smiled and pretended they hadn't heard anything, Micky's voice had echoed through the entire room.

As the night progressed, the band found themselves getting more and more comfortable. They were introduced to a few big names in the business, Jools, the male host of the show who was also the keyboard player in one of Billy's favourite bands and his co-host Paula, a petite blond with a huge personality and a big name in the media. They found themselves having their photo taken with a surly, rat faced individual with a head of tight ginger curls who had once been called the godfather of punk because he'd been the manager of the most notorious punk band of the late seventies. He stood silent and totally motionless for the picture dressed head to toe in black, a long sleeved T-shirt with knee length shorts and leggings, full of self-importance and irritation.

They were enjoying themselves so much with the free champagne and wonderful food that they didn't notice that people were starting to leave, this was obviously just an event that the celebrities attended before going on somewhere more interesting and it was becoming obvious that the band weren't going to be invited to go with them.

"Steve's just got us an invite to this because Justin and Rico were in the cab with him and knew what the tapes were," said Vince his voice full of disappointment, "I bet he got himself something else out of it, they told us he was a bit of a wide boy and full of shit didn't they?"

"It's not worth worrying about now," replied Paul, "let's just enjoy this and see what happens later. Have you seen that old woman following Micky around? She hasn't taken her eyes off him all night."

"I recognise her," said Billy, "I think my dad used to fancy her, she was really famous in the sixties."

"Fucking hell you're right," agreed Vince, "she was a top model back in the day. He hasn't even noticed has he? He lives in his own world when there's free food and drink on offer."

"Leave him to it," said Paul shaking his head, "we'll tell him tomorrow that he could have gone home with a supermodel. It'll take him a while to work out who it was and then he'll start searching the magazines when we tell him her name. It'll keep him busy for a few days."

Vince looked around the bar and saw that there were only waiters, a few people nursing drinks, and some people looking around in anticipation of someone initiating conversation with them. He decided it was time to leave, as it was still relatively early. The others agreed and as they prepared to go, they all noticed Micky was completely oblivious to the woman fixated on him from across the room.

It was warm outside in the street, there were people everywhere. Vince and Micky decided they were going to continue their evening by going to The Underworld, a live music venue and nightclub. Vince felt sure that some of the celebrities from the party had said they were going there to see an up and coming band that was playing later.

"I'm not sure you heard that correctly," said Paul, "they were all going on to somewhere in Mayfair, I overheard two of them discussing it."

"I'm going anyway," protested Vince, "there were some cool women in that party and they can't all be going to Mayfair, some of them must be staying round here and I definitely heard people talking about going to The Underworld."

"I'll come with you," said Micky checking his pockets for money, "It's too early to be going home and there's a lot of people out tonight, we're bound to find someone to have fun with."

"You two haven't got any standards," said Paul dismissively, "I'm going home, I'm not staying out just for the sake of it." He rolled his eyes in Billy's direction and marched off towards the tube station.

"What about you Billy?" Micky asked, "You going to come with us?"

"Nah, I don't fancy it mate, I think I might just go home. I've had enough tonight."

"Your loss," said Vince as he turned to cross the road, "We'll let you know how we got on tomorrow." With that, Vince and Micky strode off in search of a little more adventure.

Billy was left standing on his own in the middle of Camden, there was lots going on around him but all he really wanted was some peace and quiet and time alone. He hated the falseness and pretentious nature of the music scene. Nobody at the party tonight had really been interested in any of them, lots of people had feigned interest, wanting to know who they were and what they were doing there but when it became clear they were only there because Steve had arranged it for them, nobody wanted to know. As the evening had gone on they'd been left to talk amongst themselves, a couple of women had flirted around them but Billy had shown no interest and Micky had been more bothered about stuffing himself with as much free food as he could. Paul was in a serious relationship with a girl back in Birmingham and Vince would never commit himself to anyone too early in the evening in case he got a better offer later on! He shook his head and smiled to himself before making his way to the station. He pictured Vince and Micky leaning on a bar somewhere picking out their ideal partners for the night, he had no doubt that they'd be successful. Billy on the other hand was happy to go home alone tonight.

CHAPTER SEVENTEEN

Billy was sitting in Alicia's office thumbing through a music paper, there was just the two of them there and he could feel her staring at him. As he glanced up she hurriedly looked away and then quickly got up and made her way to the door.

"I'm going to make a coffee, do you want one?" She asked, a hint of embarrassment in her voice.

"Yes please," Billy replied, confused by the strange atmosphere that had engulfed the room. His confusion was broken when Rico suddenly stormed into the space with an enormous smile across his face.

"How are we all doing today?" He asked loudly. "I'm looking forward to the show tonight!"

Rico used to be the tour manager for Alicia's band and had since become Justin's best friend and business partner, lending a helping hand to Alicia when Justin was away performing or working with other musicians.

He'd come to the office to sort out arrangements for one of Alicia's other acts. It was the all girl band that'd appeared in the video for Someday Remember and they were playing a showcase for some invited music industry guests.

"Are we invited?" Billy asked, suggesting they should all attend to lend their support.

"Yes of course," Alicia smiled, "I'll put your names on the guest list so you shouldn't have any trouble getting in. Just ask for me or Rico if there are any issues."

"Oh cool, see you both later then," Billy said, standing up to leave them be and let them get back to work.

Later that evening Billy walked down the street towards the Embassy Club, the last time he'd been here he'd got so drunk that he couldn't remember anything about the night and had woken up with a blond girl in her luxury apartment in Holland Park. He'd got up and sneaked off home before she'd woken up. He could hear music blaring through the walls and he could see a crowd of people gathered outside, all obviously eager to get in. As he approached the door he saw Micky and Vince waiting outside with two girls each, looking very pleased with themselves. Paul was already inside, talking to members of the band about their plans and future gigs.

He made his way in and immediately felt like he'd stepped back in time. The stage was lit up in pink and purple lights and had a beautiful backdrop of stars twinkling behind it. He looked around at what seemed an endless sea of faces until he spotted Alicia standing by the door to the dressing room gesturing for him to join her. Billy made his way slowly over to her, stopping to say hello to some others and making sure he had a good view of Vince and Micky still talking to the girls they'd met outside.

Everything inside seemed electric with anticipation as the band took their positions on stage. He moved a little closer to Alicia who was smiling as she watched them perform. Everyone around them was transfixed by their performance, Billy was transfixed by one of them, Lisa, she'd been the one who he'd spent the most time with and they'd had a couple of scenes together in the video. Alicia was saying something to him but he only had eyes for the girl on the stage.

Finally, the show ended and the crowd erupted into applause. Billy was so enthralled by the performance that he almost forgot to clap along with everyone else. As he glanced around to take in the atmosphere, his gaze fell on Lisa who had just noticed him in the audience and gave him a small smile and nod.

The girls left the stage and the music roared from the in-house speakers as the night went on. Billy and Alicia weaved through the crowd to get to the bar, where it was a bit calmer. Paul joined them shortly after. Meanwhile, the girls from the band were surrounded by admirers who wanted to talk to them. Lisa fought her way through them and made her way over to speak to Billy, Alicia had been talking to him but soon moved off, leaving Billy standing there awkwardly trying not to meet Lisa's gaze. She seemed to sense it and asked if he wanted a drink.

"Yes please," said Billy hesitantly,

He followed her to the bar and they made small talk about their families before eventually getting onto music where they both discovered a shared love of old-school punk bands. They'd been talking and drinking for a couple of hours when Billy saw a woman approaching and his heart sank. He recognised her as the woman with blond hair that he'd met the last time he was here.

"Well, well... look who it is," the blond said in a sarcastically casual voice.

"Hiya!" Billy replied, trying to sound as bright as possible. "How are you? It's been a while, hasn't it?"

The blond shot Lisa a look of pity before saying, "I wouldn't waste your time on this prick. We met the last time he was in here and he was full of himself, going to be a big noise in music apparently. He came back to mine but didn't even have the decency to say goodbye in the morning; he just disappeared like the cellar rat that he is. Left me hurt, disappointed and feeling used, and let me tell you, his dick isn't much to write home about either. It's like a pencil, you won't be too thrilled when you see it."

Billy felt the blood draining from his face as he listened to the woman's words. He knew there was nothing he could say in response that wouldn't make him seem even more pathetic. He watched as the woman rolled her eyes and walked away, leaving Billy and Lisa standing there in an awkward silence.

Lisa started to laugh and Billy felt a wave of relief pass through him. She smiled at him and said, "Well, I suppose that means you won't be going home with her again tonight? Come back to mine and we can finish this conversation there."

Billy was too taken aback by the invitation to believe it was real. He nodded slowly in agreement as Lisa grabbed his hand and they made their way out of the club and back to her flat. Once they got inside, Lisa put on some music and they spent the night talking about everything from their favourite bands to their passions and dreams for the future. He was taken aback at the genuine curiosity he felt while watching her band's videos.

The hours flew by as Billy felt an unexpected connection forming with Lisa that he hadn't quite experienced before. He thought she was feeling it too from the sparkle in her eyes each time she laughed or smiled when he spoke.

Finally, Lisa leaned closer to Billy and kissed him. Stunned by her sudden gesture, he was barely able to return the kiss before Lisa grabbed his hand and pulled him towards her bedroom. Billy stumbled forward in anticipation as they reached the door. He was already aroused by the closeness and electricity between them, but suddenly he found himself unable to get an erection despite being turned on. His stomach dropped as he realised that it wasn't going to happen and he felt disappointment mixed with shame wash over him. Lisa sensed his unease and asked if everything was okay or if he wanted her to stop. Billy shook his head, feeling horribly embarrassed as he muttered, "Yes, I'm sorry."

He wanted to believe that the problem was a consequence of all the alcohol he'd had earlier that night, but deep down he knew it had more to do with the woman's poisonous words. He'd felt small, as she had belittled him in front of everyone. His face had burned with shame and humiliation as he'd vainly searched for an escape from the situation, yearning for the floor to open up and swallow him whole. It seemed like his shame was still lingering a few hours later and was still affecting him even now. Lisa gave his hand a reassuring squeeze and sat up. "It's okay, it happens to the best of us. Let's get some sleep and see how things are in the morning."

The following morning Billy woke up to find Lisa already gone, but beside him was a note telling to help himself to some breakfast and lock the door on his way out. He forced a smile as he collected his clothes and made his way home. This is what it felt like to be hurt and disappointed but it was all of his own making.

Three days later Billy found himself sat next to Vince on a train heading towards Brighton.

"I knew you had an ulterior motive for wanting those

girls in our video," Billy said with a smirk as he took a swig from the Vodka bottle that had been passed to him.

"You can talk," Vince replied harshly, "you're the one who shagged Lisa the other night."

Billy hadn't mentioned anything about his recent escapade with Lisa. He wasn't sure admitting that he couldn't get an erection would do his reputation any good at all. Plus, he was dreading facing Lisa again later, Vince had decided it would be a good idea if Billy came along with him to watch the girls band perform again as he was attracted to Laura, one of the other girls and wanted to see if she felt the same.

Billy sat in silence, feeling ashamed for the second time in a few days. He knew that what he'd been feeling wasn't due to alcohol or anything else physical, it was shame from the toxic words that had been said earlier in the night. He quickly shook off these thoughts and buried them deep down inside as he continued drinking with Vince and pretending to have a great time. He didn't have to pretend for long. They were close friends and had a great time with each other, exchanging jokes and laughter as they made their way into Brighton. When they arrived, they were ready to go out and have a fantastic night.

"We're in the wrong town mate," Billy moaned when he remembered that Lisa had said they were playing in Worthing in a few days' time. "We need to get a bus or we'll miss the show."

"It's no big deal," replied Vince, "It's only a few miles, we'll be there in no time."

"Come on then, let's find the bus stop," said Billy and the two of them set off.

An hour later they stepped off the bus having waited five minutes for it to arrive and then taking ages to get to Worthing.

"It's only a few miles," Billy sang in a sarcastic voice.

"Oh fuck off," spat Vince, "we're here now aren't we?"

"Yes mate, but I need a beer now, I'm thirsty after all that vodka and the bus journey."

Vince agreed with his friend and they sauntered off into town to find a bar before they'd look for the club that the girls were performing in.

The walk was chilly and the air was thick with the smell of fried food and the distant beat of music as the two of them stumbled up the high street with its broken, dim streetlights and stained pavements, towards a rundown neon lit nightclub near the seafront. Behind the door, two menacing-looking bouncers stood tall with crossed arms, watching everyone who walked in.

Vince pulled himself up to his full height and smiled at one of the doormen as he declared that they were on the guest list to see the band. The big man glanced at the paper in front of him without actually looking at them.

"What's the name?" he growled.

"Vince and Billy," Vince responded, trying to disguise the hint of drunkenness in his voice.

"You're not on the list," was the flat reply from the other bouncer.

"Oh for fuck's sake," moaned Vince, "They've done it again and forgotten us, is Rico around? He'll sort it out."

"He left about an hour ago," said the big man tonelessly. "Guess he'll be back when the show is about to start."

"Can we hang around inside until then?" Vince asked hopefully.

"Only if you pay first," the big man replied with a grin. "Otherwise, you can wait out here until he comes back."

"Fucking great," muttered Billy under his breath.

"Thanks anyway, mate," Vince said cheerfully, not wanting to further anger the bouncers. "We'll wait here for him."

They stood outside getting colder as they waited, hoping Rico would be back sooner rather than later. He appeared after about ten minutes and was surprised to see the two of them.

"What are you doing here?" Rico smiled.

"Didn't Alicia tell you we were coming down?" Vince said, "she said she'd put our names on the door but she must have forgotten to do it, can you get us in please?"

"Yes of course," smiled Rico, turning to speak with the doorman, "these two are with me if that's ok?"

The big man gave a slight nod and motioned for the

three of them to step inside. As they passed by, a wave of heat welcomed them from within the club.

The club was loud and crowded with people, some there just for the music, some for the drinks, some to dance and a few looking for someone to take home. Vince and Billy made their way through the throng of fans towards the bar and ordered vodka shots. The alcohol went straight to their heads as they danced erratically as Lisa and Laura sang.

The set ended after what felt like minutes but had been well over an hour and Vince and Billy took a break from dancing, getting another round of drinks before heading back onto the dance floor. They weren't quite sure if it was the alcohol or the band that caused them to make such fools out of themselves but somehow they managed to attract the attention of both girls, neither of them seemed very impressed.

Not wanting to let the chance slip away, they approached the girls and did their best to explain that they were having a great night but they'd probably drunk a little too much and asked if they would join them for drinks.

Lisa shot Billy a smirk and said, "That seems to happen quite a lot to you doesn't it?" Billy looked at the floor hoping Vince hadn't noticed anything.

Laura caught Vince's eye with a mischievous grin. "Sure," she said, "let's have some fun."

The four of them made their way towards the bar,

Vince ordered a round of drinks and they clinked glasses before each taking a sip. They drank and laughed together for another hour or so then Rico appeared and said it was time to get back to London.

"Can we get a lift home with you guys?" Billy asked hopefully.

"Sorry," Rico said, "the car's full up with four girls and their stuff, you'll have to find your own way."

"No problem," Vince replied confidently, "We'll take the train back."

"I don't think so," Lisa interjected, "it's one in the morning, there won't be anything running now. Good luck though."

With that they all got ready to leave, leaving Vince and Billy alone in what was quickly becoming an empty nightclub with no money and nowhere to stay.

"Bollocks," muttered Billy, "what do we do now? They just played us didn't they? How stupid are we to fall for it."

"Manipulative bitches," Vince spat back, already looking around for someone else he could talk to but realising that the club was deserted.

"Come on," he said, "We'll walk down to the beach, we can hang around there for a bit. It'll be morning soon and we'll get the first bus back to Brighton for the train.

The beach was quiet, the cool air welcomed them. As they walked, all the sound seemed to disappear and the only thing that could be heard was the sound of their footsteps on the stoney beach. The stars twinkled above them as they lay down and looked up into the night sky. A faint breeze blew around them.

"I can't stay here in the cold, I'm going for a walk," Vince said as he drew up his collar.

"I'm staying put," Billy answered half-heartedly, sleepy from all the drinks they consumed earlier.

Vince nodded and then strode off in the direction of the promenade until he was out of sight.

Billy lay on the stone beach for a while before finally deciding it wasn't a great idea to sleep there, exposed to the elements. He spotted an abandoned rowing boat about fifty yards away and went over to investigate. It would be much better if he could shelter underneath it from the cold, instead of lying out in the open on the beach. He stumbled across the stones until he reached the boat and climbed underneath. Surprisingly, it provided some warmth and comfort as he lay down listening to the sound of waves lapping at the shoreline. His eyes closed and he drifted off into sleep.

Billy was woken by a loud screeching noise, he stirred and crawled out from underneath the boat to find Vince surrounded by seagulls going wild as if they'd just found an all-you-can-eat buffet! He'd come back during the night and couldn't find Billy so he'd just lay down and drifted off to sleep. He tried to swat them away with his hands but it only made them angrier and even more hungry.

"Hey, do you want to help me out here," Vince yelled, still trying to fight them off.

Billy tried to suppress his laughter, before jumping to his feet and running over to assist Vince in beating away the birds. After driving them off, they both collapsed on the ground, laughing uncontrollably from the struggle.

"You idiot," Vince sighed, "you could have warned me earlier! I fucking hate seagulls."

"I didn't know you'd come back," Billy protested. "How was I to know you'd get attacked?"

"We need to get out of this place," Vince said, "That was one hell of a night!"

"Yeah, I think I speak for us both when I say that was an experience!" agreed Billy, shaking his head.

They found the bus stop just in time to catch the early morning bus back to Brighton. The journey was a quiet one, neither of them wanting to talk about the wild night they'd had. They sank into their seats exhausted, as the train pulled out of the station to take them back home to London.

Chapter Eighteen

Justin sighed as everyone gathered in Alicia's office. "Antony Weston Davies is a powerful man, and word is out that dealing with you guys isn't worth the trouble. As such, we're now having difficulty finding a label to release your single," he said. Silence filled the air as the four of them tried to comprehend why no one wanted to sign them. After all, they had already recorded their first song, made a video, planned out their promotion and tour schedule.

Justin continued, "On top of that Radio One has refused to play Someday Remember, they're not happy with the mention of sex and drugs in the lyrics."

Vince objected, "That doesn't matter though! After all, another band had their single banned recently and it became an international hit!"

Justin replied, "Yes, but that other band was already signed and well known. You guys aren't quite there yet, nobody cares if your singles are banned or not. All the other radio stations take their cues from Radio One for their playlists so it will be hard for us to get you some airplay to help promote your tour."

Micky then asked, "So what happens now? Is everything called off?"

Alicia spoke up cheerfully, "Not at all! We've received plenty of positive press about you and ticket sales have been good, there shouldn't be any empty venues. The tour should go well, some venues will pay you on the night from walk-ins. But as for releasing the single...we'll just have to find someone who's willing."

Billy piped in, "I'm sure there's someone out there who'd be willing to take a risk on us."

Justin nodded his head in agreement, "Yes, but you could help yourselves a bit more by being a little more amicable, it doesn't matter if you like the person or not, if they're someone with a bit of influence please try and get along with them. I know Weston Davies and his cronies are a pain, but you really do have to learn to control things. I'm sure we'll find a label that will take a chance. But for now, all you have to do is start rehearsing for the tour, your first show is next week!"

The four of them had mixed emotions about the upcoming tour. It was great to be playing together live again, but also quite daunting since they hadn't been on stage for so long. They wanted to make sure they were as prepared as possible for this tour. They made a promise to themselves that they'd do everything in their power to show everyone how much they'd grown.

After hours of practice and working on various pieces each day, they finally felt ready for their tour dates! They had worked hard over the past weeks fine tuning their act and getting everything ready for what promised to be an amazing show, now it was just a matter of seeing if all their preparation paid off.

Billy was up early; he'd packed up the night before so he was ready to go. He grabbed his bags and his guitar and set off to the station. They were all meeting at the rehearsal rooms to load up. He stepped out at Kings Cross straight into a heavy downpour. "I hope this isn't an omen," he thought to himself as he started out on the short walk to The Depot where hopefully the others would be waiting.

Rico was leaning against a large blue Volkswagen minibus, taking drags from his cigarette and studying an itinerary. The vehicle had been converted into a tour bus with blacked-out windows and black lettering along the sides that read "Bandwidth Trucking". As Billy got closer, he could see the side door was open, revealing leather seating around a central table, two plush benches down each side, and six bunks with thick black curtains for privacy. To the rear was enough storage for all their equipment, three seats in the front and another pull-down bunk overhead made it clear this would be their home for the next few weeks.

"Morning," smiled Billy as he stood next to Rico. "This is alright isn't it? Are the others here yet?"

"Micky and Paul aren't here yet but the others are inside, put your bags down and go and help them. I want to get on the road as soon as we can."

Rico seems a bit more serious today he thought, Billy had only ever seen him when they'd all been out together but this was obviously him in professional mode.

"No problem," Billy said, as he put his things in the back and hurried inside to find the others.

Forty minutes later the band, along with Rico, Jimmy and Fang were heading north on the A1 towards Cambridge and their first venue, The Corn Exchange. The gig went as expected, and the band felt a mixture of relief and excitement at the reception they had received. After a night of celebrating, they continued their journey. They went to Leicester and then Nottingham, before heading for Newcastle.

By the time they arrived in Edinburgh, they had developed a good routine. The shows were getting bigger and better each night and the response from the crowd was getting more and more enthusiastic.

It was around midday when they stepped off the bus in Glasgow and it was cold, damp and very overcast. After five consecutive days of all being together Billy was desperate for some time to himself. He asked Rico if he could leave and explore on his own, but before he could go Jimmy grabbed his arm, asking if he could join him.

Although Billy wanted to be alone, he thought that having Jimmy around would be useful, after all, Glasgow had a bit of a bad reputation if you wandered into the wrong area and this was his first time visiting the city. The two of them set off to explore and took to the streets, heading for some of the local attractions. As they walked along cobblestoned back-alleys, taking in the sights and sounds of the city, it felt different from all the other places they'd been to. They visited Kelvingrove Art Gallery and Museum, the Glasgow Science Centre and Glasgow Cathedral before strolling along the banks of the River Clyde to get a glimpse of Glasgow's industrial past.

"Right then," said Billy suddenly, "that's enough culture for one day, let's find a bar!"

"We've only got time for a quick one," Jimmy replied, looking down at his watch. "We need to be back at The Cat House soon."

The Cat House was the venue for tonight and Billy had been looking forward to it the most out of all the dates they were going to be playing. The two of them walked into a large pub on the corner of West Nile Street, it was filled with people all laughing and talking. Billy spotted a pool table in the corner and made a beeline for it, but before he could even start a game Jimmy tugged at his arm, "Come on, we need to go".

Billy reluctantly left the table and followed Jimmy, before they knew it, they were outside The Cat House.

They spent the next hour doing their sound check and setting up for the show. After that, they went down the road for a quick drink before heading back to the venue ready for the gig.

The night was everything Billy had hoped it would be, there were moments when he felt completely lost in music and thought he might never come back. He looked around at his friends, playing together on stage as if they'd been doing this for years. The show that night was incredible, the crowd was electric and all four of them played with a passion. Vince seemed to have the crowd in the palm of his hands and they played two encores at the end of the set, the first time that had happened on this tour. In the dressing room afterwards the four of them hugged each other and clinked bottles together in celebration.

"I need to get back out there," panted Micky as he dried off his sweat with a towel, "I know there are women waiting for me!"

"I'm coming too," said Vince, nearly pushing each other aside to get to the door. Billy and Paul just stared at each other in amazement at the show they had just played. Fang stuck his head in through the doorway and tossed them a small packet with white powder in it. "This will give you a little boost," he grinned. "It was an incredible show tonight and I think some people will want to meet you later."

Paul then fished a plastic card from his pocket and

spread two lines of the powder on his guitar case. The two of them quickly snorted it up through a banknote then Paul rushed out to join the others.

Billy stood alone in the dressing room, his mind spinning from the drugs and the excitement of the night. The moment was all he ever dreamed of, playing a stellar performance in a brilliant venue, with an enthusiastic audience. He felt as if he were in an entirely different realm. He needed it to carry on, he found himself in the centre of a crowded room, people laughing and talking and music blaring out from all directions. He spotted a woman with long blond hair staring at him from across the dance floor and signalled to her with his eyes to come closer. She was attractive enough and had an easy demeanour so Billy asked if she wanted to come back into the dressing room for drinks. She agreed without hesitation and followed him inside where they proceeded to talk for a while and then have meaningless sex in the cramped space.

Billy felt an emptiness inside as he finished up with her, he quickly got dressed again without saying another word or making eye contact. As soon as she was dressed, he grabbed her arm firmly and ushered her out of the room without even giving her a goodbye kiss or hug. He silently watched as she made her way down the stairs before turning away without giving her another thought.

He grabbed another bottle of beer from the fridge and walked over to the chair, feeling a sense of guilt as he lit up a cigarette. The women around him were loud, carefree and shallow. He looked down at himself, he was no better!

"That wouldn't have happened if I wasn't in a band," he thought. He felt like a shell of himself, hollow and emotionless. The only thing that brought him real joy was music, the alcohol and drugs were nothing more than a feeble attempt to numb the pain, but only created a deeper chasm of despair. As he smoked his cigarette, regret started to take over, regret of what he had let himself become; yet despite knowing this, he still craved more thrills and excitement and left the quiet of the dressing room to search for them.

Paul stood at the bar chatting happily with a couple of fans and Billy made his way over to him.

"Have you seen the others? He asked, scanning the room.

"They said something about going to the bus," Paul replied, so Billy made his way outside to look. As he approached the bus Jimmy was leaning on the back doors in conversation with Fang.

"Any idea where Vince is?" He asked.

Fang nodded his head towards the bus, "They're in there," he said with a smile.

Billy pulled open the sliding door and his eyes widened at the sight. A pale woman with jet-black hair and thick makeup around her eyes was writhing on one of the benches, Micky's body thrusting against hers in a steady rhythm. On the other bench a blond woman had her hands clawing at the sides of the bus as Vince pounded away violently. The air was charged with sexual energy and sweat glinted off their intertwined bodies.

"Fucking hell you two, we've all got to sleep in here tonight!" Billy shouted as he watched them in disbelief.

"They'll be gone by then," grunted Vince, barely pausing for breath as he tugged hard on tousled blond hair.

"I don't fucking believe you two," replied Billy before slamming the door shut and storming back inside to find Rico.

Chapter Nineteen

They were all unusually quiet on the bus as Rico drove them back to England. He had really shown his authority last night and left no one in any doubt that he was in charge whilst they were on this tour. He'd read them the riot act and then explained that whilst he didn't care what they did or who they were with individually, he always needed to know where they were in case they got into any problems. Everyone was expected to be respectful when it came to shared spaces like the bus or dressing rooms. All of them except Paul stayed silent with their heads bowed like naughty children, he had demanded that Vince and Micky clean the leather benches, table, and surrounding areas with cleaning supplies he'd made them borrow from the venue. His steel-eyed gaze had been enough to make sure no one disobeyed him. Everyone knew not to upset Paul; he could easily flick a switch and was capable of bouts of extreme violence. He'd never shown any aggression to any of them but they were all fully aware of what he was like and none of them wanted to be the first to be on the receiving end of his anger.

The mood lifted somewhat as they arrived in Liverpool, they all agreed to stay more focused on their music and less focused on the excesses that were part of the rock 'n' roll life.

The band had played an amazing show at The Tivoli in Buckley, then on to Cardiff and Bristol before heading back up north to Stoke and The Boardwalk in Manchester. After the performance there, a crowd of young women had gathered outside the dressing room, and the four of them enjoyed the attention. As Billy stepped outside at the end of the night, a man approached him and tapped his shoulder.

"Hey mate, that was a great show, can I have a word?"

"Yes no problem," began Billy politely before the stranger punched him hard in the face. He stumbled back, only to have more attackers approach and push him down before kicking him repeatedly from all sides. Vince and Micky came out seconds later and were immediately grabbed by another group who started to kick them while they curled up with their hands covering their heads. With so many boots trying to make contact, none of them managed to land a decent blow. Paul, Rico, Jimmy and Fang suddenly dived in to help and the gang disappeared as quickly as they'd arrived.

"That'll teach you to mess with our women," one of them shouted as they ran off, but the threat seemed to be over. None of them had been seriously hurt although Billy did have a nasty bruise forming just below his eye.

"We'll need to stop at a butchers and get a steak for that," joked Rico.

"Fuck that," protested Micky, "we're not wasting money, he can cover it up with makeup, he's got enough of it in his bag."

"Thanks for your concern," laughed Billy, relieved that it was all over. "I love you too."

"We need to get out of here now," said Paul, looking around making sure that the gang had definitely gone. "They might just have gone to get reinforcements, I don't want to be here if they come back."

They quickly got their stuff together and loaded up the bus. As they drove away, the rumble of the engine and the tension in the air mixed with the smell of leather and body odour.

Jimmy yelled, "Let's get this party bus rolling!" The music came on fast and loud, and they laughed and joked as they drove away from the scene.

The incident that night only seemed to strengthen their bond, it made them realise the importance of looking out for one another.

They drove across The Pennines to Leeds and hunted for a secure spot to park up overnight. This was the final leg of their journey, they would go on to

Sheffield, then Hull, then south to Norwich and Ipswich before the last show at The Angel in Bedford.

As the bus pulled up outside The Angel, a huge pub on the corner of the high street with a chipped sign and broken lanterns, a disappointed Micky asked, "Is this it?"

"That's what the sign says," Paul sighed from up front.

Billy shook his head, an exasperated expression on his face as he stared out of the window. "Fucking hell, what a shithole," he muttered under his breath.

Vince stepped off the bus and stretched, glancing at the pub with a slight smile. He laughed as he clapped Rico's shoulder and said, "Well, we're here now, let's get the gear in and I'll tell them they don't deserve us!" With that, he walked off towards the main entrance.

They walked inside and looked around, Rico marched up to the bar telling the barman who they were. The barman nodded to a large door at the back of the pub. "It's through there," he said, "If you need anything let me know and I'll get someone to help you. The sound guy isn't here yet, he won't be long though, and it's nearly five."

As they opened the door and stepped into the venue, their eyes took a moment to adjust from the light outside. The room was fairly big with a low ceiling and black walls; there was a huge stage at one end and a lighting gantry stretched from one side to the other.

Billy smiled, "I take it back," he said, "its not so bad after all."

"They still don't deserve us," grinned Vince, "but at least we finish the tour in a proper club."

Jimmy and Fang had already started bringing all the equipment in and they started setting up on the stage. A tall man with long black hair watched them work for a few moments before walking over to introduce himself.

"Hi, I'm Neil," he said brightly, "I'm doing your sound tonight, I'm looking forward to it, I've heard a lot about you guys."

The atmosphere changed; there was an energy about them now as they ran through a song to check levels. Once they were all happy with the sound Vince clapped his hands together then said, "Right I think we're ready to go."

They took the rest of their things to the dressing rooms before heading back out for something to eat before the show.

Returning to the venue they drank bottles of beer from their rider in the dressing room, retelling stories from their tour so far. Around 7.30pm the first few people started trickling in. They grew more energetic and the room filled out with an enthusiastic audience, by 9pm it was at capacity.

The lights dimmed as the band took their places on stage and a ripple of anticipation spread through the crowd. There was darkness save for a single beam of light that fell across Billy's face and guitar. He strummed a single chord and a pure sound echoed through the room. Paul and Micky joined in with a thunderous rhythm and music filled the air as they launched into their set.

The night was a success, as their set drew to a close the room filled with cheers and clapping, the tour was over. They'd given it their all and it felt good. They left the stage for the final time and made their way back to the dressing room, sinking into the worn out sofa and chairs as they drank what remained of their rider. They were silent as they took in the moment, knowing what it meant to them all. Suddenly, Micky sprang up, full of energy, he wanted to get out and mingle with the audience.

"Yeah!" Vince joined in, "Let's go and enjoy this. Nothing like a post tour celebration."

Billy shook his head but followed them out anyway, what could he do? As they pushed their way through the crowd to the back of the room, Vince heard someone call his name, as he turned round his gaze fell upon a woman in her late twenties with striking red hair. She smiled at him and he walked over to introduce himself. It didn't take long for the two of them to gravitate towards some secluded storeroom at the back of the club. Billy and Micky just looked at each other and rolled their eyes.

"At least he hasn't taken her back to the bus," Billy said thoughtfully, not expecting an answer as he watched

Micky approach a group of women queuing to order more drinks at the bar.

He returned to the solitude of the dressing room and talked about the tour with Paul. It had gone well and they wanted to keep up the momentum. They discussed what they thought they should do in the coming months before Rico demanded that they help Jimmy and Fang load up for the journey home. Instead of another night in the bus, he was adamant that they were going back to London tonight. The two of them were keen to pack up and go, after nearly three weeks on the road, all they wanted was a good night's sleep in their own beds with some decent food.

They all sat on the bus waiting for Rico to drive them home, he was inside collecting their money for the night, suddenly he appeared back alongside them with a troubled look on his face.

"We're not getting the full fee," Rico explained, "he says he expected more people to turn up and he hasn't taken as much as he thought he would."

"How much has he paid?" Paul asked, a hard look spreading across his face.

"£50," Rico replied.

"Well he can fuck off," growled Paul as he started back towards the pub. Fang and Jimmy jumped out of the bus and followed Paul inside.

The remaining four stood outside by the bus chatting. The air suddenly chilled as a window to the pub shattered, glass cascading on to the wet pavement like diamonds glistening in the streetlights. A cast iron barstool had been thrown through it. The four of them ran inside, expecting to be met with chaos, they were not wrong.

Inside, eight or nine regulars stood in a line against the far wall, their faces frozen in fear, Jimmy stood in front of them, his eyes cold and fists clenched tightly. To his right, Fang stood motionless with his hand inside his denim jacket, the blade of a knife glinting menacingly in the bar light. Paul had the barman pinned against the bar, pressing an arm across his throat, while twisting the other painfully up between his shoulder blades. Paul whispered something into his ear. The barman slowly nodded and Paul released him before they both moved towards a door at the back of the bar and out of sight. When Paul reappeared a few moments later, he had a fist full of bank notes that seemed to burn in the dim light.

"I think we're done here," he said quietly.

The four of them moved aside in a bizarre guard of honour as Paul, Jimmy and Fang passed between them and made their way back onto the bus.

Billy watched them go, he couldn't believe what had just happened and felt a strange mixture of disbelief and admiration. They wanted to finish the tour with a bang and that's exactly what they did.

They drove away, not saying a word, just a silent

understanding in the air. No matter what the future held, they all knew it was going to be one hell of a ride.

Chapter Twenty

Billy, Paul, Vince, and Micky arrived at Alicia's office around ten o'clock. She beamed when she saw them, her eyes brightening and her arms outstretched for a hug. Billy was fourth in line and felt the warmth of her embrace linger just a little bit longer than it had for the other members, or was it his imagination?

The band had taken a few days off after their tour had ended, but Vince and Micky had been out on the town nearly every night, keen to keep enjoying their newfound fame.

Alicia leaned forward, her voice taking on an excited edge as she revealed her news.

"I've discussed things with Justin and Rico and we've decided that we're going to release Someday Remember on our label," she started, "I've been in touch with some of my contacts in Europe and we've secured a licensing deal with a German label."

"What does that mean?" Micky questioned, "Have we got a record deal?"

"Not quite," continued Alicia, "it means that they've agreed to press a certain amount of copies, then promote and distribute them. I'm going to set up a European tour to coincide with the release date. We'll put a full package together, TV, radio airplay, press interviews etc. It means we don't have to worry about getting a record deal over here for the time being. I've already started working on it."

"Wow, that's amazing," said Vince as he sat back trying to take in the news, "when's it all likely to happen?"

"Hopefully within three months," Alicia said thoughtfully, "I'll have a better idea at the end of the week when I've spoken to a few more people."

"What do we do in the meantime?" Paul asked.

"I've got a couple of things I've arranged for you," Alicia explained. "All the artists on my label are playing an industry showcase at The Rock Garden in Covent Garden in two weeks' time and I'd like you guys to headline it. Also, a friend of mine is opening a wine bar in Gerrard Street and she wants you to be the guests of honour, you'll arrive in a limo and go down a red carpet while her photographer takes pictures. Does that sound like fun?"

"Fun?" Micky exclaimed. "A free night out with lots of gorgeous women, of course we don't mind!"

"I'm not sure there'll be lots of gorgeous women, but it should still be enjoyable. I've also booked a showcase at The Hippodrome later the same evening. You'll be on stage about midnight but you only need to mime along to a couple of songs. You'll all sing live but this is just to increase awareness around the single, it's going to be packed and we'll get a video of your performance out of it so it can't hurt." The four of them nodded, happy with the plans. Alicia had always been good to them and they trusted her judgement.

Billy smiled to himself, he was excited for the showcase and the wine bar event, but a little hesitant about the mime performance at The Hippodrome. Nevertheless, he was grateful for Alicia's efforts and knew that it was all part of the bigger picture.

As they left the office, Micky pulled Billy aside, "Me and the guys are going to head out for a bit. You in?" he asked, a sly smile spreading across his face. Billy had a feeling he knew what Micky was hinting at, a night of partying, and probably with some girls involved. He wasn't sure if he was ready to continue that kind of lifestyle just yet, but he didn't want to be left out either.

"I'm not sure," he said hesitantly.

"Oh come on, mate," Micky urged, clapping him on the back, "you're a rock star now! Live a little!"

"We seem to be living a lot lately," Billy chuckled nervously before saying, "oh fuck it why not, what time?"

He walked back to his flat, feeling a mix of emotions. On the one hand, he was excited about the upcoming events, but on the other, he was starting to feel the pressure of their newfound success. He couldn't quite shake the feeling that everything was happening too fast, that they were moving too quickly towards something that he wasn't sure he even wanted. He sat down on his sofa, deep in thought.

As the evening rolled around, Billy found himself standing inside a club with Micky and the rest of the band. The pulsing beat of the music washed over him, the bass shaking the ground beneath his feet. He leaned against a wall and watched as Vince took a swig from a bottle of vodka before passing it on to him, he put the bottle to his lips and took a large gulp, the clear liquid burning his throat. The girls around them really were beautiful, but Billy couldn't bring himself to join in. He was sure none of these girls would bother with him if he wasn't in a rising band. Fang had quietly arrived with the usual clear pouch of white powder and as the night wore on, Billy's apprehension melted away. He found himself drinking and laughing, caught up in the moment. He danced with one of the girls, feeling her body pressed against his, the smell of her hair filling his senses. He lost himself in the music, letting it carry him away. The rest of the night passed in a blur, they moved from club to club, snorting drugs, drinking, dancing and laughing. Billy felt alive, he stumbled back to an apartment with a dark haired woman who he thought was about thirty but in reality was much older. His head was spinning from the drugs and alcohol. He collapsed onto the bed, breathing heavily, his body tingling with excitement. When he woke up, he was filled with a mixture of guilt and elation. He slipped out of bed without a making a sound and left the apartment in silence. He thought about his night, reliving the moments that had felt so freeing and exciting. Everything had gone a little too far, but he had enjoyed himself and he resolved to enjoy the ride as his career took off.

It was the drink and drugs that gave Billy a newfound confidence as he ventured out with his band mates and embraced the wild nightlife again over the next few nights. He began to let himself be more extroverted, no longer worrying about what others thought. He still had moments of doubt, but he quickly moved on from them, confident that whatever was meant to be would happen in time.

Chapter Twenty-One

Lennie Ratcliffe shook their hands firmly as the band was introduced. Lennie was in the country representing a big Canadian record company and had agreed to take a look at them.

He walked around the room with an air of confidence that seemed to fill the space around him, despite his diminutive stature. He was unmistakably a force to be reckoned with, his glasses were round and had a thick, dark frame that made his brown eyes look bigger than they were. His three-piece electric blue suit fit snugly around his rotund figure, and a black silk shirt complemented it perfectly. A small gold medallion on a thin gold chain rested just below the knot of his tie, an exclamation point to complete the man's larger than life look.

"We'll get an album recorded first and get you out on a big European tour," he started, "then we'll get it released in the states. Just as it all gets going through we'll slow it down, do you know why?"

The four of them stared at him not knowing quite what to say.

"Because you'll be doing films!"

The silence and blank looks continued.

"You guys look amazing and I think you can be the complete package, we're going to have a look at you next week at The Rock Garden and then we'll firm up some plans."

Not knowing how to react, Vince stood and shook his hand, "that sounds amazing Lennie, thanks for taking the time to speak to us."

Alicia spoke up and said they should be rehearsing and told them to leave, as she wanted to speak to Lennie alone. The four of them dutifully got up and said their goodbyes before making their way out not knowing what to think about what they'd just heard.

Three days later Billy arrived at Covent Garden around 4pm, he knew he was early but he wanted a little time to take in the atmosphere before the show that evening, he wandered around taking it all in. He spotted a young couple sitting on a bench, their faces glowing with love and laughter. Billy felt a pang of jealousy, he longed for that kind of connection with someone.

He felt a grin spread across his face as he watched a group of break-dancers contort their bodies in impossible angles, their movements fluid and mesmerising. He made his way towards a street artist who was painting a portrait of a woman, her features so lifelike that it was almost as if she could step off the canvas and into the world. Billy stood there for a while, admiring the artist's skill, before moving on.

He arrived at The Rock Garden and spotted Vince.

"Did you understand what Lennie was saying?" He asked him.

"Not a clue mate," replied Vince, shrugging nonchalantly, "I have no idea what he was trying to say. I guess we should just put on a great show tonight and then maybe it will make more sense if we talk to him again."

"Glad it wasn't just me who didn't get it," Billy said with relief, "it all sounded crazy!"

Jimmy and Rico stood on the stage inside The Rock Garden, shouting out to Fang and some others as they tried to manage the chaos. Paul came over to them and said something, but Billy couldn't hear above the noise. Suddenly, Micky ran over brimming with excitement.

"All of the bands on the label are women," he exclaimed. "It's going to be a fantastic night!"

Vince stood quietly off to the side, deep in thought.

"What's on your mind, mate?" Billy asked as he went over to join him.

"Nothing really," replied Vince, before speaking again. "I was just thinking about what Micky said. He's right, all the other acts on this label are female and geared towards pop music, we're a rock band. I'm not sure if we fit in here. But maybe I'm just overthinking it, ignore me."

Vince and Billy stood in the back of the dimly lit room as the night began. There was an upbeat energy that radiated from the growing crowd, eagerly awaiting the first act. Two women from San Francisco in long, gypsy-style dresses stepped onto the stage. The sound they created was a blend of rock, folk and country, with catchy choruses hooking their audience straight away. Billy thought it wasn't quite his thing but shrugged it off. The second act emerged, a large American lady from Tennessee with long green and orange hair flowing wildly around her face and the flowing black dress she wore, she moved around the stage stomping rhythmically in enormous biker boots covered with buckles and studs. She sang in her own unique way into the microphone, captivating the audience.

Three women from Manchester were next in line to perform. As soon as they began, it was clear that something was wrong. The lead singer's voice sounded strained and the other two seemed so out of sync that by the second song people had begun to trickle away from the stage. The trio finished up their last few songs feeling embarrassed and inadequate.

"The sound system wasn't loud enough," Billy heard one of them say to a friend as they bought drinks after they'd finished their set, "and I think we were just a bit too nervous about performing in front of such a big crowd."

Billy felt terrible for them but didn't speak; his eyes went back to the stage where Lisa, Laura and the rest of their band had begun their performance. The four girls sang in unison, their voices bouncing off one another like four birds in harmony. The crowd began to cheer and clap along as the band increased the tempo, and soon bodies were swaying around to the music. The four of them moved around the stage energetically, they hopped from side to side, encouraging people to get up and dance whilst others nodded their heads in approval. Their set was electric; everyone was clapping along in time with the beat. The Innocent were now under pressure to perform!

The atmosphere was intense as everyone's eyes were glued to the stage. The Innocent played song after song in quick succession making sure that each one had its own distinct sound and feel, when each song finished there was huge applause showing just how much people were enjoying their performance. They kept playing for over an hour, the crowd went wild when they finished their closing number and left the stage. Billy loved this feeling; he loved playing rock 'n' roll!

They sat in the dressing room after the show as Lennie burst in through the door followed by an excited looking Alicia.

"Guys you are amazing," he gushed, "I'm going to get

on the phone as soon as I get back tonight, I'm recommending that the label offer you a deal as soon as possible. You've really blown me away with that performance."

They all just looked at each other not knowing what to do, Billy felt numb but Vince suddenly hugged him, "we need to celebrate," he screamed, "Micky, pass us some drinks please."

Lennie shook each of their hands before promising that he'd be in touch soon. When he'd gone Alicia joined them and settled down next to Billy with her drink.

"That was great," she said, "you guys were fantastic up there!"

Billy finally smiled, "thank you," he replied in disbelief. Alicia then clinked her glass against his bottle before drinking it in one go. The others soon left the room leaving Billy and Alicia alone with each other. She turned to him with a smile on her face, asking him about different things in his life. With every question he answered she learnt more and more about him as well as how important music was and why being part of this band meant so much to him. He felt at ease in her presence, like he could open up about some of his deepest thoughts and feelings without judgement or worry. As their conversation continued they began to laugh. It felt good for Billy to be able to talk without worrying what people might think of him, here in this dressing room with Alicia he felt free!

Rico appeared out of nowhere and Alicia quickly put some distance between herself and Billy, he said that Lisa was asking for him in the bar and Billy thought it was the perfect time to escape, he wasn't sure what had happened just now but he knew that he had to be careful.

He made his way out into the main room, Lisa was talking to Paul but when she saw him, her face lit up with a huge smile. She made her way over to him and began telling him how much she'd enjoyed the show and maybe they could meet somewhere afterwards to continue the night alone. Billy's mind instantly returned to Worthing, he and Vince had been left stranded after spending all their money buying drinks for the girls who'd hinted at spending the night with the two of them. Now here she was wanting to use him as a ladder to get a bit closer to the fame she craved. He looked her up and down before turning her away, rejecting her advances.

He found himself talking to the lead singer of the band from Manchester; he couldn't help feeling some sympathy for her after their performance earlier.

"I'm sorry you didn't get the reception you were hoping for," he said.

"Oh don't worry, it was just something we needed to experience," she replied. "It's not every day that a band like us gets to play in London."

They spent the rest of the night chatting, and then she asked him if he'd like to walk her back to her hotel.

He followed her up to her hotel room where she took out her keys and opened the door allowing them both inside. Billy was standing there, present in the moment, but his thoughts were somewhere else entirely. He couldn't stop thinking about what had happened in the dressing room earlier with Alicia. He couldn't get her expression out of his head.

CHAPTER TWENTY-TWO

"I thought we were getting a fucking limo," shouted Paul angrily, as he stood in the doorway to Alicia's office building before joining the others out on the pavement. The four of them stared in disbelief at the dark green Citroen CX Prestige that sat in the street in front of them, its hydropneumatic self-levelling suspension waiting to spring into action as soon as the ignition was turned.

"Is this our limousine then?" questioned Micky, disappointment etched across his face.

"Look, a cars a car isn't it?" snorted Vince, opening the back door and sliding across the plush leather seat, "we're getting a lift into town so just get in and deal with it."

Billy hopped in next to him, he wasn't really interested in what type of car they arrived in, he was excited for the evening to start.

Paul and Micky climbed in reluctantly but their spirits brightened when they saw the fridge full of ice-cold beer. They each took a bottle and settled back to enjoy the ride.

The vehicle stopped at a single entrance in Gerrard Street, close to Chinatown in Soho. Two blue neon strips framed the sleek metal door, more subtle than the pink neon doorways that illuminated the seedy peep shows and bars further down the street.

Vince stepped out of the car onto a ratty red rug, splayed out on the pavement in an attempt to create a makeshift red carpet. He held his shoulders back, looking every inch a star as his three band mates followed him out. Alicia hung back, happy to be part of the group but not wanting to draw too much attention to herself. A photographer appeared and asked them to pause so she could take some pictures for a magazine that was covering the opening.

They stepped inside, eager to escape the cameras and the embarrassment that they felt. They found themselves in a mirrored entrance hall, with shimmering silver walls lit by soft light bulbs that reflected their uneasy expressions as they climbed a sleek, metal staircase. Vince led the way and when he reached the top, his eyes widened at the sight of an ultra modern wine bar. The room glistened with polished surfaces and high stools, while leather sofas filled the wooden floor and glass tables overflowed with trays of bubbling champagne.

The band settled into a comfortable booth, soaking in the lively atmosphere of the bar. Billy was sipping on vodka and coke when he noticed Alicia making her way towards them with a tray of champagne flutes.

"Hey guys! I thought we could celebrate with some bubbles," she said, handing out the glasses.

They clinked their glasses together before downing the champagne in one go. Billy felt a buzz as the alcohol hit his bloodstream, the warmth spreading throughout his body.

The night swept by in a blur of drinks and laughter, Billy couldn't help but notice how Alicia kept looking at him, her eyes filled with something that he couldn't quite place.

Rico tried to get everyone focused on the show they had to put on in an hour, but Paul was too tipsy to take it seriously.

"We're just miming," he slurred, "how hard can that be?"

"I still need you to be professional," Rico replied. 'I don't want any of you ruining the progress we've made recently."

Vince shocked everyone by agreeing with him, "no more drinking till after the performance," he declared, then he strayed off to the other side of the room where an attractive dusky-skinned woman was holding a microphone.

Billy stood at the top of the stairs next to the balcony;

he was enjoying a moment to himself when Vince wandered over to join him. As he did so, he stumbled and spilled a glass of red wine down into the stairwell. When they peered over the guardrail, they saw an angry face belonging to a famous black actress who was currently appearing as a matriarch in a primetime soap opera. The expression on her face could have come straight from her television role. The two of them froze as she marched up the stairs towards them, not knowing what would happen next, but when she reached them, she burst into laughter and introduced herself as Sally with a cheerful greeting that neither of them had expected. "Well," she said, "I've never been greeted like that before!"

Billy and Vince exchanged a look of relief before introducing themselves to Sally. She seemed genuinely interested in them and even offered to give them some advice if they ever needed it. They talked for a while longer before Rico called them over; it was time for them to leave for The Hippodrome.

They ambled their way to Leicester Square, with Rico believing that the chill of the night air might help them shake off some of their drunkenness. But when they got there, it seemed to have had the reverse effect. They were taken up to their dressing room on the fourth floor; Jimmy and Fang were already there with their instruments. Fang also had something special for them!

As they were enjoying a drink before the show, there

was a knock at the door. A tall man wearing ridiculously tight black jeans, high-heeled Chelsea boots and a glittering black shirt underneath a shiny red jacket with a top hat and a silver cane stood waiting for them. He introduced himself as Christopher. He held a dog lead that was attached to a collar around the neck of a dwarf who wore tails and an undertaker's gloves but no shirt. The whole scene was bizarre!

"It's going to be a wild one," Christopher began in his camp drawl, "and you darlings, are the stars of the show. I'm your compare for the evening. Hold on to Barney here whilst I visit the boys room."

He handed the lead to Micky and flounced off down the corridor. Micky pulled Barney inside and immediately pushed him into the store cupboard at the back of the room. He turned the key before smiling and heading out into the corridor. "I'm not a fan of dwarfs," he said, "it won't hurt him to be in there for a few minutes, I'll let him out when we've finished."

They all watched on in amazement but were too stunned to argue, they followed Micky out and ran into Christopher as he returned from the toilet. "Where's my boy?" he cried, before rushing into the dressing room in search of his friend. The band continued down the stairs in search of the stage. They found themselves in the basement surrounded by beer kegs, ancient records, outdated lighting cans, and decrepit speakers, they were lost!

"How the fuck do we get out of here?" exclaimed Paul, "If we miss the show Rico's going to kill us!"

"Over here," cried Micky as he noticed a patch of light above them. The stage in The Hippodrome rose up from beneath the floor and they'd found it just in time. They stepped onto it as it rose up into the arena.

The crowd cheered in delight as the band members emerged, the backing track played and although it felt very alien to them, they managed to pull off an amazing show. As they left the stage Christopher was there, holding Barney on a lead as if nothing had happened. The dwarf had a strange look in his eyes, like he had just witnessed something terrible. Billy started to feel uneasy, unsure of what was happening.

"Great show, darlings!" Christopher exclaimed, "Barney here couldn't get enough of it."

Billy couldn't shake the feeling that something was off. He watched as Christopher led Barney away, wondering what kind of person would subject another to that kind of treatment. As they made their way back to the dressing room, he couldn't help but feel like they had just taken part in something that was just a little too weird.

"I'm really going to have to quit the drugs," Billy muttered as they sat in their dressing room. "I could've sworn I saw a dwarf on a lead earlier."

"Yeah, it's certainly been a weird one," Paul agreed. "Let's go downstairs and pretend we never saw it. Rico said we're allowed in the Star Bar tonight since we're not being paid for this show. I wouldn't mind grabbing a drink right now.

The Star Bar sat just left of the main entrance to the club and was reserved for celebrities looking for some privacy from fans or other people who wanted to bother them. As they walked past the burly bouncer, they found an empty table tucked away in a corner. They settled down and ordered drinks.

Vince and Micky strolled in with a girl on each arm. "I can't believe they've been out there already," groaned Paul, "It's like being in a band with a couple of old dogs on heat."

Billy couldn't help but laugh. He was relieved to be in a place far away from the craziness that had just taken place outside.

The DJ was playing some old-school punk rock, the air was thick with smoke and after a few drinks everyone's worries began to slowly evaporate. The rest of the evening went by relatively peacefully but Billy had seen enough, he unsteadily got to his feet and said his goodbyes to his friends before he stumbled outside in search of a bus stop. He bought himself some food from a street vendor and waited for the night bus to take him home.

He was jolted awake by a rough shaking on his shoulder, and opened his eyes to see a short, stubby man in a bus driver's uniform looming over him. Billy looked around, realising he'd dozed off and missed his stop. He felt the grease and chilli sauce seeping into the fabric of his shirt from the half-eaten kebab that was still lying on his chest. "What time is it?" He asked groggily, "Where am I?" "3am," came the reply, "you're at the bus station in Streatham, first bus back into town is at 6.07 but you'll need to wait outside the station, they lock up when all the buses are in."

"For fucks sake," Billy muttered to himself and he stepped off the bus and into the cold street outside, he threw the remains of the kebab in a bin and pulled his leather jacket tight around him. He found a bench opposite the station and sat down to wait for morning and a bus back. This wasn't the first time this had happened, he decided that he wouldn't be getting a night bus again!

Chapter Twenty-Three

Billy listened to Justin's static-filled voice through his headphones as he spoke from the control room.

"You nailed it," Justin said, sounding thrilled, "that one was perfect, come through and have a listen for yourself."

Billy put down his guitar and went to join the others who were standing behind the huge mixing desk listening to their latest song.

They'd been at East/West Recording Studios for two weeks now because Lennie Ratcliffe was insisting that Earthlines would be signing the band up once all the paperwork had gone through. Justin, who would soon be leaving to work in New York, had offered to use some of his own studio time to begin recording their album. He said that if they could get all the recordings done before he left, he could book another studio to mix and master it when he came back. He was willing to wait for his fee until the record deal had been finalised.

Vince and Micky put in long hours everyday, then would hit the town at night. Paul and Billy were a bit more laid back but still enjoyed going to clubs at the weekends or maybe one or two nights during the week. Alicia ensured their names were on all the guest lists at all of the places they liked to visit, so they didn't have to wait in the long queues with everyone else. They had access to all the special areas that celebrities usually frequented, although most really famous people rarely came to the places they visited.

Billy was impressed with how their latest song was sounding. He could feel the buzz of excitement in the room, knowing that they were creating something good.

"See, I told you guys we were destined for greatness," Vince said with a grin, slapping Micky on the back.

Paul rolled his eyes but couldn't help but smile. He knew they had something special with this band.

For the next ten days, Justin painstakingly guided the band through each step of the creation process. His skilful guidance and unwavering focus helped them create a stunning album that they hoped would soon become legendary.

"I think that's all for now," Justin said as he stood to stretch, "and I'm pleased with what we've recorded so far. I'll be heading off to New York soon – hopefully when I return, the deal with Earthlines will have gone through and we can get back into the studio to mix these tracks. I'll take a copy of the recordings with me to have a few listens while I'm away. We've got great potential here, I believe this album is going to be something special!"

The band members hugged each other, relieved and exhausted but also filled with a sense of accomplishment. One by one they left the studio.

"Don't forget about tomorrow night," Justin shouted as the studio door shut.

"I'm looking forward to it," Vince replied, beginning to walk down the stairs.

"Are we going for a drink?" Micky asked. "After all that work, I think we should," he suggested.

"I don't want to go into town now," Paul said.

Billy agreed with him, saying, "We have a big night planned for tomorrow so I'm going home." He started away towards the tube station.

Micky muttered under his breath, "Fucking lightweights." His eyes were filled with disappointment when Vince also announced he was leaving.

"Guess I'll see you tomorrow then," he said glumly before turning around and searching for a nearby bar where he could have a drink alone.

Billy stepped out of his flat at eight o'clock the following morning and began to make his way down the street. He had only walked a few steps when he heard heavy footsteps behind him. Startled, he wheeled around to find a tall, muscular black figure looming above him.

The man wore a hoodie that cast a deep shadow over his face, and Billy could just make out the glint of metal in one hand.

"Give me your money," growled the stranger, and then with a menacing flick of the wrist he brandished what appeared to be a small switchblade. "I haven't got any," replied Billy, palms up, trying his best to appear truthful. "You must have..." said the stranger. Fear bloomed in Billy's chest as he watched the man's index finger tighten around the knife.

He began to talk, telling the stranger about his dreams of becoming a professional guitarist and how he had just come from the studio last night where they were working on something special. His voice trembled as he relayed stories of the amazing progress made throughout the weeks. Tears pooled in his eyes as he discussed the ambition of one day making it big and achieving something with substance. He even promised that if, by some miracle, they got signed, he would use whatever fame or fortune came out of it and give back to those less fortunate who needed it most. He knew he was babbling, but he was frightened.

When Billy finished speaking, he looked up at the stranger expecting violence or aggression like before, instead what met him was sympathy and understanding emanating from deep within the hooded figure's gaze. After a few moments of quiet contemplation, the man eventually lowered his knife and looked away saying simply: "Go home." Then without another word turned around and walked away.

Billy exhaled slowly in relief, his heart racing as though it could burst right out of his chest at any moment. He tried to convince himself that this chance encounter had taught him that sometimes all you need is a bit of courage and faith to turn a situation around, no matter how frightening or daunting it appears. Deep down he wasn't so sure.

Rather than stay outside, exposed in the street, he quickly headed back to his home. As soon as he reached its safety, he let out a huge sigh of relief at the thought of being safe from whatever had just occurred.

He spent the rest of the day playing his guitar with a certain detachment and then chose to engross himself in a film as the afternoon wore on. After showering and getting dressed for the evening, he stared at himself in the mirror and was suddenly overwhelmed by fear at the thought of walking to the train station.

He needn't have worried, as the short walk was uneventful. He jumped on a train heading northbound and settled down in a seat at the end of the carriage. He arrived in Wardour Street, making his way to the Ship pub that had been chosen as the meeting spot. Vince was already there, one hand feeding coins into a fruit machine while he balanced a pint of lager in the other.

"Hey," Billy beamed as he joined him, "how long have you been here?"

"Oh, a couple hours I think," He responded, "I won £40 but most of it went back in! You want another drink?" Vince offered him some money.

"Of course," said Billy as he gulped down his beer, "give me five minutes and I'll go to the bar."

Just then, the fruit machine lit up with winning sounds and started spitting out coins in its collection drawer.

"Woohoo!" roared Vince with joy, "bring us both a chaser too. Let's celebrate this win together."

Billy grabbed the coins from the fruit machine and walked over to the bar. As he waited for the barman to pour the drinks, he noticed a group of rowdy men in the corner, their laughter and volume increasing with each passing minute. Billy felt his unease growing. Suddenly, he felt a hand grab his shoulder, nearly causing him to spill the drinks. Billy whipped around to find a large, imposing man glaring down at him.

"Hey! Blondie! You got a problem?" the man slurred.

"No," Billy spat back, trying his best to keep his composure.

"I think you do," the man growled. "This is our pub, we don't want queers in here."

"Fuck off," Billy replied, "I'm just getting my mate a beer."

The man and his group didn't seem satisfied with that response. They began to taunt and jeer at Billy, their aggression escalating. Suddenly, Vince appeared at his side, sensing the danger.

"Everything okay?" Vince asked, his voice dripping with faux bravado.

The man looked Vince up and down, analysing him and his intentions. Micky and Paul suddenly appeared and stood next to their friends. After a few silent moments, the man finally nodded and backed away, leading his group to another corner of the pub. Vince and Billy breathed a sigh of relief and clinked glasses in celebration.

"You saved my ass there," Billy said, feeling grateful.

"Always got your back," Vince said with a smile. "Now let's enjoy the night."

"What the fuck was that all about?" Micky asked as Paul made his way to the bar.

"Nothing mate," Vince said quietly, "just our resident trouble magnet here."

"I can't help being beautiful," laughed Billy, tossing his hair theatrically.

The four friends decided it might be a good idea if they left and found somewhere else and before long they were all enjoying themselves in The Intrepid Fox, bouncing around to the music and drinking vodka shots.

CHAPTER TWENTY-FOUR

"What time is it?" Paul yelled over the music to Micky.

"10:30!" Micky shouted back, barely audible in the loud bar.

"We need to leave," Paul continued, "Justin made it clear that we shouldn't be late." He then began gathering the group together. All of them made their way out of the crowded bar and into the street. Vince complained as he followed, saying he was having a great conversation with a beautiful woman and didn't want to leave.

"You might want to look at her next time you're sober?" Paul questioned as he walked off.

The group started across Soho Square when Billy announced that he had to piss and ran into some nearby bushes. "Me too," Paul added, attributing it to the cold air. When they reached the entrance of the square, rushing to catch up, they noticed Vince and Micky sitting inside an open-top Mercedes that sat in one of the parking bays.

"Get out of there," Paul yelled, "cameras are probably all around here." Despite his efforts, Vince couldn't start the car without any key, so he got bored and hopped out. "Thought we could turn up in style," he laughed as he began walking again. Paul just looked up to the heavens and rolled his eyes before following him.

They strutted to the head of the long line outside The Hippodrome and were let in without a word by the two enormous bouncers standing guard.

Justin and Rico were already at the bar inside, The Star Bar. Justin saw them entering and gave a friendly wave as if to say "You're just in time," then he nodded his head toward Rico, who had just started buying drinks for everyone. Billy glanced around the room, spotting Alicia at a table with two other familiar faces that used to sing with her band. She smiled and waved at him.

Rico brought the drinks over; they each found their own spot as they gathered around talking eagerly about the band they were going to see tonight. Billy couldn't help but notice how Alicia and Justin seemed very distant from each other, it seemed like there was tension between them. He managed to push any thoughts from his mind as they continued talking; it was nothing to do with him.

At midnight, everybody in the packed club was looking eagerly up at the stage. A famous five, a drummer and keyboardist from a group based in Manchester, a bass player from one of the loudest heavy metal bands in the world, plus a guitarist and singer from an American superstar band from New Jersey had taken their places. Billy couldn't believe the atmosphere, he was standing just feet away from these incredible musicians. At the front of the crowd, hands reached out to touch their idols, and he wondered what it must be like standing on that stage, receiving such adoration.

After the band performed four songs to loud cheers, it took a while for the applause to die down. Billy and his friends followed Justin back into the seclusion of the Star Bar, where they discussed the show. Justin quickly introduced them to the bassist, drummer, and keyboard player as they walked into the bar, he seemed to know everybody. The band spent some time with the three of them before they were whisked away to meet other fans eager to talk to them.

Billy thanked Justin for introducing them when he suddenly smiled at him and said quietly, "come with me," and the two of them left the room before anyone noticed they were going.

Justin led Billy up the stairs and through a door and suddenly they were high above the club in an area that had luxury booths and intimate seating. Billy could see a group of people at the far end chatting and drinking as they sat and looked down at everyone dancing and singing on the dance floor below. Justin led Billy towards them and the huge security man stood forward, Justin nodded at the man, who nodded back and allowed them both in. Two of the group stood immediately, warm smiles on their faces as they greeted and shook hands with Justin. They exchanged a few words then Justin turned to Billy and said, "meet Jon and Ritchie, I'm sure you know who they are!"

Billy was stunned, these two were in one of the most famous bands in the world and here he was shaking hands and having a drink with them. 'Hi," he managed, trying to be as composed as he could but he felt star struck, "That was an amazing show, absolutely brilliant." Jon and Ritchie both thanked him for saying so and then chatted with him for a while, asking him about his own band and what he hoped to achieve. Billy couldn't believe how normal the two of them seemed, he felt as if he was talking to two of his mates in the local pub. They spoke for a little longer then he felt as if he had taken up too much of their time and left, thanking them for taking the time to speak to him.

Billy yanked the door open and was surprised to see three women waiting at the top of the stairs. They were all dressed the same, mini skirts, high heels, tight tops and cropped leather jackets with long, flowing fringes, they looked like triplets. One of them stopped him by putting her hand on his arm as she spoke up: "are you with Jon and Ritchie? Could you take us to see them please?"

Billy smiled politely as he told them, "I can't, I don't think they're allowing anyone else up there."

"Oh please," she said while running her fingers through her thick black hair and pushing her body into his. She stepped closer and continued, "if you could get us upstairs we would go somewhere else afterwards and have a great time together, if you wanted?" She pouted her lips and winked at him as she spoke.

"Where do you have in mind?" Billy asked quietly.

"Two of us share a flat in Camden. We could all go back there and have some fun," came the reply with another flirtatious wink from her heavily made-up green eyes.

"Are you saying that all three of you will sleep with me if I help you get up there?" He grinned while asking the question.

She smiled confidently as she answered, "We really want to meet them so yes, if that's what it takes."

Billy shook his head and pushed past them as he walked down the staircase, "fucking slags," he muttering under his breath, amazed at the lengths some women would go to if they wanted to meet famous people. Disappointment etched the faces of the three women who still lingered at the top of the steps.

Paul and Alicia were together with her friends when Billy arrived at the bar. After getting himself a drink, he sat down next to Alicia. She nudged closer to him and he felt her fingers brush across his inner thigh. Ignoring the gesture, he launched into his story involving the three women on the stairs.

One of Alicia's friends cut in, "That's just part of being famous. People were all over us when we were in the charts, men and women." She smiled nostalgically as she thought about it.

"It's exciting for a while," Alicia added, "But you get sick of it, people don't see you, they only see your fame."

They chatted for a bit longer but Billy was feeling uncomfortable sitting this close to Alicia with everyone around. He mentioned that he was going to search for Vince and see what was happening. He finished his drink and stood up to leave.

He found Vince with Micky as they stood near the exit talking with some girls. As he stood with them, Billy saw two of the women from earlier strutting towards the exit. They glowered at him as they drew closer and fuelled by all the alcohol he'd consumed, Billy couldn't resist taunting them, "Good night ladies," he said smiling, "Jon and Ritchie send their regards," his tone dripping with mock politeness.

"Fuck off, you poser!" one of the women snarled viciously, her lips curling into a sneer. She spat in his direction and a thick glob of snot landed on his leather trousers just below the knee.

"How delightful... your mother must be very proud," he replied sarcastically despite knowing it would only spark further rage. The two women responded with twin middle fingers and a string of obscenities. He snapped back with a pretentious kiss blown in their direction before taking a napkin from a nearby table. Billy wiped away the spittle from his trousers as he seethed silently with rage. He was developing a real dislike for the women in this scene!

"Are you making friends again?" Micky said through his smile.

"I don't know what you mean," was all Billy could reply as he poured something from a glass onto the napkin and continued to clean.

He stomped back to the bar, replaying the event in his mind. The club was now nearly empty, and Alicia stood alone in the doorway. He slid onto a corner table and lit a cigarette, drinking vodka from a glass with a shaking hand. As he sat there brooding, Alicia walked over to him; she pulled him into a tight embrace before pushing her lips onto his. Her left hand slid down to his crotch, teasingly squeezing before she suddenly pulled away as she whispered "we'll continue this soon" then she ran out into the night to join her friends who were waiting in a taxi outside.

Billy sat alone, reflecting on the events of the night,

"What the fuck has just happened?" He said to himself, "this has been one strange night." He looked up as Paul shouted to him from the doorway. "We're getting a cab home if you want to join us?

Billy couldn't get into the car quickly enough, he needed to get home to try and make sense of what had happened tonight.

Chapter Twenty-Five

Billy stepped off the tube and onto Kings Road, walking in the direction of Alicia's office. Two weeks had gone by and the band had been rehearsing for their first European Tour. He was glad to see Vince and Rico already there when he arrived, as it meant he wouldn't be alone with her. He'd been avoiding her ever since that night at the Hippodrome and had only spoken with her on the phone a couple of times since then.

"Hey, come in and take a seat," Rico said, gesturing toward a comfy sofa. "Have a look at these before the others arrive." He then handed Billy some papers filled with the tour itinerary.

"There's twenty-two dates here," Vince noted as he skimmed over the sheet. "That'll take its toll on my vocal chords, I might have to make sure I'm taking better care of myself on this one."

"If you like mate," Billy smiled; they both knew that

Vince would be relishing all of the extras listed in their riders and hotel accommodations.

They carried on flicking through the pages as they heard the office door open. Billy could feel a lump appear in the back of his throat as Alicia stepped in. She greeted them with a smile, before quickly glancing in his direction. He felt a chill run down his spine. He was glad when Rico broke the silence, pointing out some of the tour dates.

"So, we'll have a few days in Holland, and then a couple of weeks in Germany, before finishing up in Paris." Alicia explained. Billy tried to focus on what she was saying, but he couldn't help feeling uncomfortable under her gaze.

"The ticket sales have been great, and the press we've sent out has had a good reception," she continued. "People are already really excited about you, so hopefully it will be a successful tour. You'll have hotels booked each night and the tour bus for transport during the day, Rico will give you an allowance for food and whatever else. Matt will make sure you're getting the right sound out front and Gary will be doing the stage lighting, but you'll need to work with the in-house guys to get your onstage sound just how you want it. The release date for 'Someday Remember' is day you play Hamburg, so it should be an amazing show!" Alicia paused to take a deep breath before continuing. "Oh! And I almost forgot, there's a lot of airplay for the song, so it looks like it's going to chart when it comes out!"

Micky was the first to jump up from his seat after hearing that last piece of news. "Fucking hell yes!" he shouted.

The remaining three then got to their feet and hugged each other in pure joy. They knew the hard work and heartbreak of recent years was finally going to pay off.

"Have you heard anything from Lennie yet?" Vince inquired when everyone had settled down. "It's been two months since we last spoke to him, does it really take that long to finalise a contract?"

"Justin asked me the same thing when I talked to him earlier this week," Alicia responded. "He's over in New York for six months and he wants to know when he should reserve studio time to mix your album. He was also worried about when he would get compensated for all of his past work. We've already put a lot of funding into setting up the tour but because sales have gone so well, everyone stands to make something from it so we're not too concerned about that. I received a draft copy of the deal, but I sent back a revision. That being said, no one has got back to me yet. When you're done with the tour, we'll be able to finalise things and move forward."

Vince seemed satisfied with the explanation for now, but Billy could see worry in his eyes. They both knew that two months was a long time to put together what should be a typical first contract.

"So let's get out of here," Micky said as he stood up. "We've got work to do for the tour!"

They all stood up and followed him out of the office; Billy's heart was pounding as he stepped out onto the street. The tour was finally starting; they'd be on the ferry to Holland in two days time. He was also looking forward to getting out of London and away from Alicia. It seemed they were never going to get past the awkwardness of that night, but at least now he could focus on the positive. With any luck, the next few weeks would be filled with the buzz of the road and the excitement of a new adventure.

The night before the tour, Micky gathered all four of them for a last minute practice. Even though they were tight as ever, it was more a chance to get into the ideal mind-set for the upcoming weeks. After three hours of gruelling practice and a couple of drinks, they were ready for Holland.

The first night in Rotterdam was a massive success! While backstage, they had all been nervous, Billy had heard the buzz from the huge crowd packed right up against the stage. Vince had been pacing around the dressing room but then Micky had taken it upon himself to step out first and touch all the hands that had been offered up to him, instantly a roar had come from within the audience which had put them all at ease. With the intro music playing, they'd stepped out on stage as if it was second nature to them. The performance had been electrifying, Micky and Paul started off with a thunderous beat, and the crowd began bouncing along to the rhythm. When Billy added in his guitar, everyone seemed to go wild. Vince's singing drove the energy even higher and the band kept the energy at its peak throughout their performance, and when they'd completed their set they'd been called back for two encores before leaving in exaltation and then collapsing in the dressing room in pure elation.

Jimmy and Fang came in to join the celebration of the first night's success, Fang bringing with him a packet of white powder he'd acquired that evening.

"Do you know people everywhere?" Vince asked as he leaned forward to grab the small mirror on the table in front of him. Fang just smiled back at him, revealing the hole left by his missing front teeth.

"I hope so," Billy said, "We'll need something to keep us going if the other shows are like that one."

"Can we go outside and join in with the fans?" Micky asked Rico, who was watching with slight apprehension from the back corner.

"Yes," he replied, "but I'd prefer it if you stayed around the bar area rather than going off alone into the main club, I can't keep an eye on all of you, and I don't know what might happen if you wander off by yourselves."

The four of them exchanged a knowing glance before heading out, followed closely by Fang and Jimmy. Rico watched with concern as they made their way through the club towards the main bar area outside.

The scene outside was hectic, with people dancing in all directions and the music blaring. Billy turned to see a group of five women all smiling at him, they were dressed in short skirts and leather jackets and their eyes sparkled even in the dim light of the bar area. It became clear very quickly that these ladies had taken quite an interest in him as well as each member of his band.

He smiled back at them. Before long he was talking to a woman named Anna, she had very long blond hair with sparkling blue eyes and she wore a tight fitting and rather low cut top that let her impressive cleavage show.

The drinks went down quickly, leaving everyone in the bar with a lightness to their laughter and conversation. Every now and then, Billy made his way back to the dressing room for another hit of cocaine. Rico suddenly appeared and declared that it was time to go to the hotel.

Micky had given out the name of the hotel and when they arrived, a group of women were waiting for them. They continued their night by drinking in the hotel bar until it eventually closed, and then they moved up to their rooms on the fourth floor.

Billy reached out to take Anna's hand, hoping he could lead her back to his room. But she pulled away.

"I'm going with Vince," she said coldly.

The rejection sent Billy into shock, "I thought we were having a good time," he said sadly. "Why are you choosing him? He hasn't even spoken to you all night."

"My friend Beatrice is with him now," she replied, her eyes searching for her friend. "We're both going to be with him tonight, he's the singer, he's more important than you."

Billy was speechless. They had enjoyed themselves so much at the venue and then in the bar downstairs, yet now Anna was choosing Vince because of his status as lead singer.

"Are you serious?" Billy asked, disbelief flooding his expression. "Do you want to sleep with whoever has the most status?"

Anna gave him a pitying look as she walked away towards Beatrice who was about to enter Vince's room.

Billy was shocked by the events that had taken place in the corridor, amazed at the woman's shallowness. He stumbled into Fang's room where he found him and Jimmy having a beer. They offered Billy one as well and a line of white powder that Fang had made ready for them. They talked, drank, shared stories, and listened to music until Jimmy announced it was almost five o'clock and he was heading to bed. Billy got up slowly before saying goodbye and wandering back to his own room. Three hours later, Rico was banging on his door telling him it was breakfast time downstairs and they'd be leaving in an hour.

They finished breakfast and collected their belongings then the four of them were on the tour bus with the crew heading from Rotterdam to Amsterdam in preparation for the second show of their tour. Exhausted after a night filled with alcohol, drugs and partying, they all piled into their bunks for some much needed sleep. Rico woke them at four o'clock, demanding they get ready for their sound check. If every night was going to be like last night, it would be a long tour indeed!

Chapter Twenty-Six

The sound check went smoothly, and the band was feeling good about the upcoming show. They were gaining a reputation for putting on an electrifying performance, and the word had spread across Europe. Fans were lining up outside the venue hours before the doors even opened; eagerly waiting for the chance to see them perform.

The Amsterdam show was nothing short of magical. The crowd was bigger and more energetic than the night before, and the band fed off that energy. Micky's drums were pounding, and Paul's bass was thrumming. Vince's voice soared through the air, and Billy's fingers flew over the strings of his guitar. The way they played that night was nothing short of legendary, and they knew it. As they wrapped up the last song of their set, the crowd began to chant for an encore. They couldn't disappoint, and so they stepped back out onto the stage.

But the encores didn't stop at just one or two songs. They played three and the crowd still wanted more. It wasn't until the band realised they had played every song in their repertoire that they finally had to let the audience go. The cheering and applause as they left the stage was thunderous, leaving the band with a feeling of pure euphoria.

As they made their way back to the hotel, they were met with a small group of fans waiting outside. They seemed to be waiting specifically for the band, and when they saw them, they rushed over with intense excitement.

One girl in particular caught Billy's eye. She had bright pink hair and was wearing a black leather jacket covered in pins and patches of all sorts. Her eyes were wide with excitement and when she began to speak, Billy couldn't help but take notice of her accent.

"Hey, you guys were amazing tonight!" she gushed, her words rolling off her tongue in a thick Dutch accent. "I've been waiting to see you for ages, and you did not disappoint."

Billy smiled at her, trying to catch his breath after the excitement of the night. "Thanks, we really enjoyed it."

She gestured to the hotel. "Do you guys want to take us up to your rooms and party for a bit?"

Billy looked around at the rest of the band, who all seemed to be in agreement. The girls followed them up to their rooms where the night took on a similar theme to the night before, lots of drink, drugs and empty chatter. Eventually it was time for bed and Billy thought why not spend the night with her. He didn't particularly care one way or the other but she was there and he may as well take advantage of that. Regardless, he had no respect for these women; they only wanted to be able to boast that they'd slept with someone from the band.

The rising sun heralded the end of another wild night, and he was filled with conflicting emotions. He woke her up and told her he had to leave. He hadn't realised it then but his actions made him seem cold and uncaring but the girl's smile never faded, it only seemed to grow wider as she watched him go.

Vince was waiting outside for him, looking as if he hadn't slept in days. "Ready to go?" He asked with a knowing grin. The answer was yes; it was time to move on to the next city and the next show. So off they went, the sounds of their last performance fading away into memory as they drove further and further away from Amsterdam.

The tour continued in the same way, sound check, show, drink, drugs, party, sex and sleep all day whilst Rico drove to the next city. Billy began to think more and more about his actions as he lay awake in his bunk and how it could impact his life moving forward. He realised that as long as he kept living like this he would continue having these empty moments with no real substance or worth behind them. Although he knew this was a mistake, the thrill of joining in with the partying was too strong to resist. Once the show ended, he barrelled forward without hesitation despite his own misgivings about what was happening.

Eventually, after nineteen days on the road the band finally arrived in Hamburg. It was the day of their single release, and they couldn't be more excited for it after all the hard work they had put in over the past few months. As they drove into the city, signs around town showed that people were already aware of their music and there were posters advertising their show tonight. When they reached the venue they stood in awe looking out at how many people were waiting outside despite only being early evening! They found out that tickets had sold out within days of going on sale, much quicker than anyone had anticipated since it was a smaller release than usual. Everyone seemed so eager to see them play!

After their sound check, Vince said he was going to take a trip to The Reeperbahn.

Micky looked at him in confusion and asked what it was.

"It's basically Hamburg's version of Soho," Paul replied with disdain. "No matter where you are, a hooker's a hooker! If you think it'll be different here, have fun. I'm staying here to relax before we play."

Billy remained quiet, not wanting anything to do with those women. They reminded him of the night he'd been attacked back in Soho. He couldn't stand what they represented and wanted to keep his distance.

"You can go as long as you keep Jimmy with you and do exactly what he says when it's time to come back," Rico commanded sternly. "Remember why you are here, to further your music careers, not look at prostitutes!"

Vince nodded, though Billy could tell he wasn't really listening. He was too caught up in the excitement of exploring a new place. Billy decided to stay with Paul and relax before the show.

After a few hours, Vince, Micky and Jimmy stumbled back into the venue, looking dishevelled and out of sorts.

"How was it?" Billy asked, though he already knew the answer.

"Amazing!" Micky slurred, throwing an arm around Vince for support. "Those German girls really know how to party! No, I'm only joking, it's just like Soho but with German accents. "

Billy couldn't help but shake his head and roll his eyes. He knew Vince and Micky were only interested in the thrill of the moment, and not the connection or meaning behind it.

As the night went on, the band played to an ecstatic crowd who sang along to every word of Someday Remember. There was an amazing energy in the room and it was clear that their music was resonating with people on a deeper level. For Billy, it was a turning point.

He realised that the true passion and meaning behind his music was more important than any short-term thrill he could get from partying and meaningless sex. He vowed to make a change and put everything into his music moving forward.

The tour continued, but this time Billy was different. He still enjoyed drinking and partying, but he no longer felt the need to constantly pursue the empty thrills of the road. He eased back on the drug taking and distanced himself from the shallow woman that hung around after the shows, that was until the final night of the tour in Paris!

The final show was a resounding success, the audience on their feet clapping and shouting for an encore. As they took to the streets of Paris afterwards, there was electricity in the air as Vince led them from club to club. The night descended into a haze of intoxicating drinks, drugs and beautiful women weaving in and out of their arms. Back at the hotel, things only got wilder, they drank more alcohol, drugs were consumed, wild sex ensued, screams and laughter echoed across rooms until finally everyone fell asleep exhausted from their exploits.

In the morning they slowly gathered around for breakfast sharing stories of their adventure while Rico ran around making sure they were all packed up by check out time. After loading up for the journey to the ferry port, they took one last lingering look at Paris. The doors to the bus slammed shut and they were on their way back to London, it had been an unforgettable experience that left them wanting more.

But for Billy, the events of the night had left a sour taste in his mouth. He couldn't help but feel guilty about the way he had acted towards the women and how he had let himself get caught up in the moment. As the bus made its way towards the port, he sat quietly in his seat, lost in thought.

It wasn't until they had boarded the ferry and found a quiet spot on the deck that he finally spoke up.

"Guys, listen. I know we've had a wild ride these past few weeks, and there's no denying that we've had some incredible experiences. But I can't help but feel like we've crossed a line, like we're not really living our lives with purpose."

Vince looked at him quizzically. "What are you talking about? We've been doing what we love, playing music and having a good time."

"I know, and that's great. But what I'm saying is, I want us to do more than just party. I want us to create something real, something that means something to us and to the people who listen to our music."

The band stared at him in confusion, Micky said, "You're always looking for the deeper meaning in things. You'll be ready to rock and roll again after a few days at home. We just had an amazing tour and our singles in the charts in Germany so take a moment to appreciate it all. I'm not changing anything yet."

Billy shook his head. "No, it's not about changing anything yet. It's just about being more intentional with our actions and not giving into the temptations of the road so easily. We have a responsibility to ourselves and to our fans to create something meaningful and authentic."

Vince nodded slowly, understanding Billy's perspective. "I see where you're coming from. And you're right, we do have a responsibility. But at the same time, we can't take ourselves too seriously. We're still young and we're still living life. It's about finding a balance."

Paul spoke up for the first time, "I agree with Vince. We need to find a balance but you're thinking too deeply about it. Just enjoy it all while it lasts."

The rest of the ride back to London was spent in quiet contemplation. Billy was still grappling with his thoughts and emotions, but he knew that he was heading in the right direction. The tour had been a wild ride, but it had also been a wake-up call for him. He didn't want to live his life in a blur of parties, drugs and one-night stands. He wanted his music to mean something and to connect with people on a deeper level.

As they arrived into London, Billy felt a sense of purpose. The tour may have been over, but the real work was just beginning.

Chapter Twenty-Seven

Billy was jolted awake by the sound of the phone ringing in the hallway. He jumped out of bed, pulled on some joggers, and raced down to answer it.

"Billy, is that you?" came Alicia's voice from the other end.

"Yeah, it's me," he replied groggily, "what time is it? I just woke up."

"It's 11:30," she informed him. "We all need to meet at 2 o'clock. I'm going to call everyone else now, so make sure you're here on time."

He hung up the receiver and shuffled back up to his flat. They'd only been home for a day and already Alicia was calling an emergency meeting. Why couldn't they have at least one day to themselves before having to get together and discuss stuff?

Rico opened the door to let Billy in, where Vince and Paul were already sitting in Alicia's office.

"Let's wait until Micky gets here and I'll tell you what's going on," Alicia said, organising her papers into an orderly pile on her desk. "Rico here has been telling me about your recent adventures," she smiled, "It's normal to be a bit wild on your first tour, you'll probably calm down during the next one."

"I wouldn't count on it," Paul muttered in response, "they get pretty crazy when they have had too much to drink."

Billy wasn't sure if Paul was referring to him and Vince or if it was aimed at Micky and Vince, but he decided not to think too deeply about it.

Just then Micky rang the intercom and Rico went to let him in. When they all sat together in the office Alicia began.

"We have a problem," she declared with a solemn expression on her face. "Earthlines are bankrupt so there's no record deal. Lennie was loosely associated with them but shouldn't have made any offers of contracts. Justin is livid and has lost studio time and money."

Micky asked, bewildered and dejected, "What does this mean for us?"

Vince snarled, "Didn't you check Lennie out? That should have been your first priority."

"He seemed so genuine." Alicia defended herself, "I really believed he was legitimate. Clearly I was wrong."

"What do we do now? Vince countered, "Is there anyone else willing to sign us?"

"Listen, Vince," Alicia began, "Someday Remember is in the charts in Germany, Denmark and Finland so we need to keep the momentum going and capitalise on your success there. I'm looking for someone to finish the album so we can licence it again."

"What are you talking about?" Vince snapped back, clearly irritated by what she was saying. "If we're doing well in the charts, why isn't the German label able to pay for the album to be finished? They should be able to back us up with all the success we've had."

"The thing is," Alicia reasoned, "they don't have a lot of resources. But if we manage to get the recording finished soon, they'll be happy to licence it again. Justin has already said he's not putting any more money into it. He feels as let down as you guys do, and things between him and me are tense right now because of it. We'll just need to restructure the company to make it work."

Alicia took a deep breath and continued, "We can't afford to wait for money from a label. We need to do something else if we want to tour Europe again."

Paul leaned forward in his chair, "What did you have in mind?" he asked curiously.

"I've been talking with the same promoters from some of the major cities," Alicia began. "They are willing to sponsor another tour. We'd need to do some smaller gigs around Germany and Scandinavia but it would pay for itself. There seems to be a lot of interest out there so I think we should take advantage of it while we can."

The four of them looked at each other, their faces lighting up as they discussed plans for another tour to Europe.

After about three hours, Vince and the others left the office, with Vince having voiced his opinion on the matter. Despite their disagreements, they were all excited about getting back out on tour. They were also invited to perform at a couple of Europe's biggest music festivals. Tensions had eased towards the meeting's end, and Alicia had mentioned that her friend was throwing a party at The Embassy Club that night. Billy felt apprehensive, remembering two prior embarrassing visits to this location, but this time he looked forward to going out with his friends again.

That evening Vince, Paul, Micky and Billy arrived at the Embassy club. Billy was a bit quiet at first, but soon he started talking with the other guests and even decided to try his luck on the dance floor.

The band was doing what it usually did on a night out; they drank too much, snorted copious amounts of cocaine and flirted with abandon. Micky and Vince left with a group of women they'd been partying with, while Paul left with his new girlfriend, they'd met just before the tour had started and she'd been invited to the party as his guest. Billy, meanwhile, had become lost in the fog of booze and hadn't noticed how much time had passed until he came back from the toilets, having gone in there with Fang, and found most people had left the party. As he went to say goodbye to Alicia, she grabbed his arm to stop him from leaving whilst she said goodbye to her friends.

"Want to share a cab?" She asked Billy, but he just stood there fixed in a drunken smile.

They stepped outside and the warm air blew against Billy's face. He almost fell over until Alicia grabbed him and steadied him. She hailed a black cab and they both climbed in. It took about thirty minutes before they arrived at her apartment in Chelsea. On the way, Billy was consumed with laughter; he was in such a good mood. Alicia paid for the taxi then, linking arms with Billy, they stumbled up the steps to her front door. When they entered, the two of them crashed onto a plush red leather sofa that occupied a large chunk of the living room wall. As he surveyed the room in his foggy stupor, Billy noticed packed bookcases, framed gold discs from Justin's song writing, pictures of him with the artists he'd written for, extravagantly decorated furniture, and faint lighting that illuminated various pricey items throughout the place.

"Let me get us something to drink," she suggested. "Is there anything you fancy?"

Billy grinned mischievously as he responded, "Yes... But I shouldn't."

Alicia smiled before she got up and disappeared into

the kitchen, only to come back with a bottle of vodka and two glasses. She knew exactly what Billy had meant by that. She just smiled, took his hand, and pulled him up the stairs to her bedroom.

When morning came, Billy found himself in her bed, alone. He was horrified by what he had done and couldn't remember exactly how they got there. He tried to gather his thoughts but all he could remember were flashes of the night before, laughter, dancing, conversations and Alicia's face lighting up as they discussed plans for another tour to Europe.

Billy didn't want to jump to conclusions but he had a feeling that this may be one situation that would not have a happy ending. After gathering his clothes, Billy quickly made his way out of the apartment without being noticed. On the walk home he continued to ponder what could come from this night, but he didn't want to think about it anymore. The hours spent with Alicia were some of the most enjoyable times Billy had experienced in quite a while, however his conscience was weighing heavily on him, all he wanted was to simply disappear into thin air.

As the days passed, Billy tried to push the night with Alicia to the back of his mind, but it kept resurfacing again and again. It was all he could think about. He was ashamed of his behaviour, but also couldn't help feeling a pang of regret. Alicia was a beautiful woman, and he'd enjoyed spending time with her. But he knew that he couldn't keep hiding from the consequences of his actions, and he needed to face things head on.

The band had a rehearsal scheduled for that afternoon, and Billy dragged himself there, feeling the weight of the night's events still pulling at him like a weighted vest. He walked into the rehearsal room, and the others greeted him with a friendly wave, oblivious to the internal turmoil he was facing.

They launched into their first song, and Billy tried to lose himself in the music, but it was no use. His playing was off and he couldn't focus. After a few minutes, Vince stopped the band abruptly.

"What the fuck is going on, Billy?" he asked, his tone accusatory. "You're playing like shit. Did you go on another bender last night?"

Billy could feel the eyes of the other band members on him, and the shame he felt was almost overpowering. He swallowed hard, and steeled himself for what he knew he had to say.

"Look... Vince... Guys... I've fucked up," he stammered. "I... I spent the night with Alicia. And I'm sorry."

There was a stunned silence in the room, and Billy could feel the heat rising in his face. He knew he'd taken a huge gamble telling the band.

But then Paul stepped forward, and clapped him on the back. "It's okay mate," he said. "We're your friends, we get it." Vince nodded in agreement.

"You shouldn't have done it," he added gruffly. "But

we won't judge you, Paul and I both went with Sarah Morton so we can't really say anything can we?"

Billy sighed in relief, he was far from feeling better about what had happened, but at least he'd told the band about it. They launched into another song, and for a few minutes at least, Billy managed to leave his worries behind and just enjoy the music.

But the weight of his actions continued to linger in the back of his mind, like an itch that wouldn't go away. After rehearsal, Billy got the tube home, not really sure where to go or what to do.

His flat was dark and quiet, and he couldn't shake the feeling of loneliness that had settled over him. He poured himself a drink and sat down on the sofa, his mind wandering uncontrollably.

But then he heard the phone ringing out in the hallway, his heart started pounding. He hesitated for a moment before finally answering.

"Hello," he said, trying to keep his voice steady.

"Hello yourself," Alicia replied, her voice warm and familiar. "I was wondering when you were going to call me."

Billy felt a knot form in his stomach. He didn't know what to say to her, or how to explain what had happened.

"I'm sorry about the other night," he finally managed. "I shouldn't have.....I mean, it was a mistake."

There was a long pause on the other end of the line, and Billy held his breath, waiting for her response.

"I know it was a mistake," Alicia finally said, her voice softer now. "But I don't regret it, Billy. I had a good time with you."

Billy didn't know how to respond and he heard himself saying, "I don't regret it either, what do we do now?"

There was a few seconds of silence before Alicia spoke again. "I think we should talk about it in person. Can we meet up later?"

Billy hesitated, but a part of him wanted to see her again.

"Of course, where do you want to meet?" he asked.

"Let's meet at Blushes on the Kings Road," Alicia suggested. "I'll meet you at 8pm."

Billy agreed and hung up, feeling a mix of nerves and excitement in his stomach. He spent the rest of the afternoon in a daze, going through his daily routine but unable to really focus on anything.

When 8pm came, he found himself standing outside the entrance to Blushes, his heart beating fast in his chest. He spotted Alicia approaching him, her red hair blowing in the wind, and felt a jolt of desire run through him.

"Hey," she said, giving him a small smile.

"Hey," Billy replied awkwardly.

They made their way to a table in one of the corners and soon after a waitress arrived to take their order. As they sat there, an unspoken tension hung heavy between them. They spoke politely but avoided addressing the elephant in the room. They avoided eye contact but the tension between them only grew. Alicia finally looked up at him and smiled, quickly finishing up their drinks, they left the bar in a hurry and headed back to Alicia's home.

CHAPTER TWENTY-EIGHT

Billy perched on the edge of the stage at Verti Music Hall in Berlin, watching as sound engineers and technicians made last minute preparations for the band's performance. He contemplated what his future would look like when this tour ended. Eight nights on the road had taken them from Belgium to Germany, where they'd already put on six shows. Tomorrow, they would travel on to Denmark for two more nights, then back to Germany for a festival appearance before finishing their tour in Hungary.

The band was fantastic on this tour, tighter than ever, with each member seeming to feed off the energy of those around them. Vince's performances had been especially impressive, he seemed to be pushing himself and dragging the others up with him. The after show parties were energetic affairs too, full of booze, drugs and partying. Vince and Micky usually went off with different women but Paul and Billy had abstained, Paul had his girlfriend waiting at home and Billy wasn't sure if it was thoughts of Alicia that held him back or something else entirely. Either way, music was so much more important to him than anything else.

As the venue began to fill up with fans, Billy felt the familiar rush of adrenaline. He picked up his guitar and started to warm up, his fingers dancing across the strings as he practised a few scales and chords.

The lights dimmed as the crowd roared, and Billy felt his heart hammering in his chest. He could see the faces out there in the darkness, all the people who had come to hear them play their music. It was a humbling feeling, and he felt a sense of responsibility to give them the best performance he could.

The first notes of their opening song rang out, and Billy launched into his part with all the passion and energy he could muster. The crowd responded in kind, surging forward and singing along to every word. Billy felt himself slipping away from reality and into the music again, the outside world falling away until there was nothing left but the sound of his guitar and the voices of the crowd. They played for nearly two hours, moving through their repertoire with seamless ease.

Backstage, he collapsed onto a sofa, his muscles aching and his throat raw. The rest of the band joined him, high fiving and hugging each other in celebration of another successful show.

"Fuck yeah!" Vince exclaimed, a grin plastered across his face. "That was incredible!"

Paul nodded in agreement, his eyes shining with the adrenaline of the performance. "We killed it," he said, clapping Billy on the back.

Billy looked around at his band mates, feeling a sense of camaraderie and brotherhood. They had been through so much together, and the bond between them was unbreakable. He smiled, feeling grateful for their friendship and the music they created together.

As the four of them toasted their success with Micky handing out beer, Vince pouring shots of vodka, and Fang cutting lines of cocaine for each of them, Billy took a moment to reflect. He would drink and take drugs to excess again. The thought of having to talk to people outside his little group horrified him. All the stupid questions bored him, but he knew he had to be there for the fans and go through the motions. He had grown to detest the easy women and groupies who were just trying to sleep with anyone in the band or crew. After the show was over he just wanted to escape, but they were all in it together so he had to stay and put on a face for their fan base. Getting completely wasted was the only way he could manage it.

As the night wore on, Billy found himself getting lost in the haze of alcohol and drugs. He felt a sense of detachment from reality, as if he were watching everything happen from a distance. He saw Vince disappearing into a back room with a group of women, Micky snorting coke off a table before rushing to join him; Paul was on a payphone in the corridor outside to his girl-friend back home. Fang sat beside Billy, cutting up another line of coke before offering it to him.

With a sense of resignation, Billy took the drugs and snorted the line. He felt the familiar rush of euphoria, followed by a wave of numbness. It was a cycle he had repeated many times before, a way of escaping from the pressure and expectations he felt.

As the night wore on, the party grew more intense. Billy found himself surrounded by women, all vying for his attention. He tried to talk to them, to connect with them in some way, but their conversations felt hollow and meaningless. He knew that none of them really cared about him, that they were only interested in his fame and success.

As the sun began to rise, Billy stumbled through the slick streets of Berlin, feeling emptiness in his heart. He knew he couldn't keep living like this, that he needed to find a way to break free of the cycle of drugs and alcohol. But he didn't know how to do it, and the thought of facing the world without those crutches terrified him.

As he stumbled back to the hotel, he felt guilty. He lay down on his bed and stared up at the ceiling, Rico pounded on the door, shouting that they had to be ready to leave by 8am. Billy's relationship with Rico had been strained on this tour, and he couldn't explain why, he thought that maybe Rico suspected something between him and Alicia, he would be right! They had been seeing each other before the tour started. Even though he knew it was wrong, Billy couldn't bring himself to stop. He planned on sorting everything out when the tour was done, everything was a mess and there was no way that it could go on.

The day after, they drove west into Denmark. The whole tour was an endless cycle of long days and even longer nights. They would sleep on the bus all day as Rico and Jimmy drove. They returned to Germany for the festival. There were bands from all over the world in the tented village backstage. A rock band from Sheffield challenged them to a game of football, Billy and Vince scored goals for fun but that was mainly due to the other band's one-armed drummer being in goal. After performing their set they had to take a few moments just to process everything. Billy couldn't believe how many people he'd played to, it seemed like a never-ending sea of faces and hands. The same thing happened the following day in Hungary at another music festival. On their way back home on the tour bus, Billy and the band couldn't believe how well it had gone, they felt elated by the experience, so excited that they never wanted it to end. They agreed to meet at Alicia's office in two days time to find out when they would finish recording their album and what would come next.

They arrived at Sloane Square and made their way to the office, which was all locked up.

"Where did she go?" Paul said exasperatedly, "there's usually someone here."

"You have to give her a ring," Micky suggested and nodded towards Billy.

Billy walked back into the tube station and used a payphone to call Alicia at home.

"Hey, it's me," he began with a cheerful tone, "where are you? We're all here at the office but it's locked up, are you alright?"

Alicia sighed heavily. "I was hoping to talk to you, I tried calling you earlier but no one answered. Justin and I have broken up. He was financing everything for the company, so now I've had to move to new offices. I'm moving out of my apartment by the end of the week and Rico won't even talk to me...it's a total disaster."

Billy responded sadly: "I'm really sorry about that. What should we do now? How should I tell the rest of the band?"

Alicia seemed a bit frustrated as she replied: "I can't think right now, just go home and I'll call you later."

Billy relayed the news of what had happened when he got back to them.

"I knew something like this would happen," Vince said when Billy had finished. "We needed a new manager anyway, she isn't right for us. She specialises in female pop groups and if she can't get us a record deal while we're charting in Europe, then she can't have the right connections."

Billy felt a bit of loyalty to Alicia since she'd secured them a licensing deal in Germany, got them out on tour, and into the charts.

"We should get rid of her," Micky joined in. "Justin has all the money and contacts, he's got the album recorded and he's got the masters so she's no use to us now."

"Maybe we should take some time to think it over," Paul proposed, attempting to reason with everyone. "Let's go talk about our options and come up with a plan."

The band agreed that they needed to think about it and headed out to discuss what next steps they could take. As they sat in the dimly lit bar, their conversation drifted from Alicia to who they thought could manage them and get their album finished. Billy couldn't shake the feeling that they were moving too fast, that they needed to slow down and focus on the music rather than the business side of things. He brought it up to the group, but no one seemed to agree with him.

Vince was already on his third drink and slurring his words. "We have to keep pushing forward. We're on the edge of something big here, we can't just stop and take a break."

Micky nodded in agreement, "Yeah, we can't lose the

momentum we've built up. We need to keep touring, keep recording, keep pushing ourselves."

Paul, who had been silent for a while, spoke up slowly. "I don't know guys, maybe Billy's onto something. We've been on the road for weeks now, and we're all exhausted. Maybe we should take a break and come back to it with fresh eyes and ears."

The group fell silent, each lost in their own thoughts. After a few moments, Vince leaned over the table, "You're being too dramatic, we're a rock band, we need a proper manager, I think we should get rid of her, I'll speak to Justin and see what he suggests."

Billy knew that it wasn't worth arguing when Vince was in this mood, he was a strong personality and at the end of the day it was his band, he was the singer after all. He decided he might as well stay silent and wait to see what happened in the coming days.

Chapter Twenty-Nine

Later that night, Billy laid in bed, staring out of the window, the moon casting a glow across the room. He couldn't shake the feeling that they were making a mistake and that he needed to take control of his own life. He turned over, facing the wall, and closed his eyes, trying to will himself to sleep. He couldn't help but think about Alicia and the way things had ended between her and Justin. He felt guilty for having feelings for her while she was still with Justin, but what would happen now that they had broken up? He knew it was wrong, but he couldn't help the way he felt. He decided he would go and see her in the morning.

The next day, Billy made his way to Alicia's apartment. He needed to talk. When she opened the door, her face softened and she invited him in. They sat in her living room, neither of them saying a word yet the silence between them felt more comfortable than anything they had shared before.

Finally, Billy spoke up. "I know things have been messy lately... with you and Justin breaking up, and our album..." he trailed off for a second before continuing, "But I wanted to know why you're with me?"

"I don't know if we're together, Billy," she muttered in a soft voice. "I feel something when you're around and I want to get to know you better, I want to understand why you can change from the lovely, polite young man you are normally to the nasty, unpleasant character that appears when you drink or take drugs. It's like being with two different people and I'm curious about it, that's all."

He was baffled by her words. "So do you want us to keep seeing each other?" He asked, now embarrassed that he appeared to have got everything wrong.

"Yes, I think so," she answered hesitantly. "I enjoy spending time with you but your band mates may not be so keen on me. Vince doesn't seem to like me very much."

"It's not that Vince doesn't like you, he just worries that you don't have the contacts we need," Billy explained.

Alicia glowered angrily and moved away from him, facing out of the window. "How dare he say something like that!" She spat out. "Look at all the things we've accomplished since I started managing you."

"They think that has more to do with Justin," he

replied quietly. "Now that the two of you aren't together, they're unsure what will happen next."

"I'll tell you what happens next," she said angrily, "you don't get any more help from me, you're on your own."

"That didn't come out like I meant it to," Billy tried to explain.

"I don't care," she snapped, dismissing him with a wave of her hand, "you need to go now, I'll talk to you later."

Billy left the apartment feeling like he was a naughty child who had just been scolded by his teacher. He took the tube back to Clapham and found a bar on the high road; he bought himself a drink and settled in the corner as he lit a cigarette. Everything seemed to be falling apart and he couldn't understand why.

Billy, Vince and Micky met in The Ship, the air between them tense. Vince and Micky had come to confront Billy because Alicia had told them what he'd said in her apartment a few days before.

"What have you been saying about us?" Micky asked aggressively, "Are you trying to screw us over?"

"I haven't said anything about you," Billy countered, "We were getting rid of her anyway so it doesn't matter does it?"

Micky went on, "We need to find someone else to manage us first. You've messed it up by telling her too soon, did you think you would get something else out of it?"

"What are you talking about?" Billy yelled back as he stood up menacingly.

"You know what I mean," Micky shot back, "you've changed recently, all you wanted was to be with her and not on tour with us."

"That's bollocks Micky and you know it," Billy defended himself angrily, "What am I supposed to do, just fuck groupie slags every night and not think about the music?"

Micky grabbed the front of his jacket and shoved him against the wall. Their faces were inches apart as he spoke through gritted teeth. "You're not interested in being with us anymore, you want to do your own thing."

Vince jumped in between them and pushed them apart. "Calm down," he said, "it's not his fault Micky."

Billy moved away and screamed back at them angrily, "You can all fuck off! I'm sick of playing the rock star; I want people to take me seriously. I'm leaving, find yourselves another guitarist." With that last statement he stormed out of the pub and down the street away from them. He wasn't sure if this was the correct decision but he knew one thing for sure, he wasn't going to change his mind.

Billy sat uncomfortably in Alicia's new offices on Cromwell Road, underneath the Hammersmith flyover.

Her assistant, Lauren, a dumpy little woman with a pig-like face, clearly disliked him. Billy had stayed at Lauren and her partner Julie's place once before when he and Vince didn't have anywhere else to sleep. They'd spent the night in her dining room. However, when they woke up in the morning, they realised that their heavy smoking had killed Julie's goldfish by depleting the oxygen from its bowl. Julie was devastated, and Lauren had asked them to leave. They'd found refuge for the night on Richmond golf course where they slept on a bed of moss between the fourth and seventh fairways until a golf ball crashing off a tree early in the morning had exposed them, forcing them to make a run for it. It was obvious that Lauren had a real dislike for Billy since she'd found out that he was seeing Alicia, he assumed that she wanted to spend some time with Alicia herself, he'd seen the way she looked at her.

"What are your plans now?" Lauren asked him as they waited for Alicia to turn up.

"I'm thinking a few days away, then see if Alicia can help me with recording some music of my own," he replied, trying to be amiable.

Lauren was quiet for a few moments and then suggested, "If you like you could both join Julie and I, we're going down to Kent for the weekend with her parents. It might be fun and they always welcome guests."

"That sounds terrific," Billy said excitedly. "Let's ask Alicia when she gets here, see what she thinks?"

When the four of them stepped off the train at Deal on the Kent coast, Julie's father was waiting for them. Andrew was a handsome man, with thick white hair and a warm smile; he looked very similar to Billy's father Alastair. He shook Billy's hand firmly and kissed Alicia lightly on her cheek, his hand lingering on the base of her spine.

The little white-walled cottage where they were heading wasn't far from the beach. Roses climbed up the garden wall, and azaleas and daisies lined its edges. Helen, Julie's mother, stood there with a tray of champagne flutes filled with golden bubbles. She greeted them warmly in a very tight pink top and a black skirt that split down one thigh to reveal her shapely leg.

As they got to know each other in the tranquil environment of the garden, Helen disappeared to the kitchen occasionally to prepare dinner. As they ate and talked politely, Billy felt something in the atmosphere. Afterwards, while sipping a glass of wine on the patio, Andrew pulled up next to him and began speaking. He moved on to talk about Alicia, mentioning how beautiful he thought she was. Billy wasn't sure what Andrew was implying, but it seemed as if he was suggesting some sort of romantic connection between the two of them. He even added that Helen had told him how attractive she found Billy.

Billy was uncertain how to react, so he decided to take a few minutes to gather his thoughts. He made his way to the bedroom where he and Alicia would be sleeping, it was Andrew and Helen's room but they were insistent that the two of them take their room for the night. They had said that it was much more comfortable than the guest room and happily offered to sleep there themselves.

As he reached the top of the stairs, Billy couldn't resist the open door, and he put his head inside the door to the guest room, he was shocked by what greeted him. He stood for a moment, stunned by the items on display. A pair of handcuffs dangled from the headboard, and leather straps quivered at regular intervals along each side of the bed like an enormous spider's web. On each wall, a collection of rubber masks watched him with deep black holes for eyes, and a selection of sex toys were arranged neatly on the dressing table alongside other objects that looked like they could cause serious pain. Billy had no idea what this was all about. He rushed from the room in shock.

Two hours later, he was talking to Alicia in the garden. He had finally managed to get her alone.

"It seems a bit strange here, don't you think?" he started, gesturing towards the family gathered on the patio, "they all seem a bit too....friendly."

"I know what you mean," she nodded, "Helen came straight out and asked me if I wanted her to join me and you later with, erm… our activities. It appears that they're swingers."

Billy's earlier suspicions were confirmed, "What did you tell her?" He asked nervously.

"No thanks, politely of course," Alicia said.

Billy sighed in relief and exclaimed, "Thank god for that! They look like my parents, it's all too much for me!"

"We should make our excuses and go to bed soon, then leave after breakfast tomorrow," Alicia smiled. "I'm fine with whatever people do in their own home but I have no interest in taking part"

"Let's make our excuses now and get off to bed," Billy suggested. "The sooner we get away from here the better."

For the next four months, Billy would spend time with Alicia every so often. She had moved out of her apartment and was staying with different friends until she found a place to call home, although occasionally she would spend the night at his place. However, he found himself preferring those times when he was alone in his own space, without someone constantly around to disrupt his routine. He had recorded four songs on his own, and Alicia was using her connections to try and get him a record deal. He missed playing music with his old band mates, and he couldn't help feeling that leaving them had been a mistake, a feeling that only grew stronger as time passed.

"I spoke to Antony Weston Davies," Alicia declared

one day when Billy asked if anyone had shown any interest in his music.

"I know he's interested in me but I wouldn't sign with him if he had the last label on Earth!" Billy replied with disdain.

"You should think about it Billy," she stated firmly. "There doesn't seem to be any alternative and it would benefit me as well."

"What do you mean by that?" Billy asked, "Would be happy for me to prostitute myself to an old queen like him? Are you just using me like you used Justin to build up your management career?"

Alicia was speechless at first, then she tried to speak, but Billy cut her off.

"I've been a complete idiot, haven't I?" He spoke more to himself than to her, "I really thought you cared and we had something together but you're just like everyone else here in this shitty music scene. Vince was right about you!"

"What the hell does that mean?" Alicia retorted, anger rising within her.

"He said you didn't have any real contacts of your own. I might not be in the band anymore but at least I've worked it out before I got too close to you. Fuck me I've been a complete prick! It's over! Have a nice life!" he spat while looking her up and down. He shook his head sadly and walked away, leaving Alicia standing alone.

Outside in the street, Billy contemplated how

quickly everything had unravelled; it was only a few months ago that he'd been playing to thousands of people across Europe with a song in the charts. He walked in silence and deep in thought, he knew he needed to make some big decisions.

CHAPTER THIRTY

Billy was sitting opposite Barry Marlow in Barry's fifth-floor office in the DCS Records building. Billy had managed to get past the receptionist downstairs, bringing with him a demo of his music.

After listening to the last track, Barry looked up at Billy and said, "So, what do you want me to do for you?"

Taken aback by the question, Billy smiled and blurted out, "Give me a record deal and make me a superstar!" Barry replied with a smile, "That's what everyone sitting here says, what makes you think you have what it takes?"

Billy composed his thoughts and told Barry about his former band's success in Europe and how he had co-written many of their songs. He emphasised to Barry that he only wanted an opportunity to continue what he had started. Barry nodded approvingly and said, "I like your stuff, Billy. But I need to see your new band perform live, let me know when you have your next gig and I'll try to come along." Slightly deflated but still hopeful, Billy thanked Barry for his time before reassuring him that he would let him know when the next show was coming up.

As Billy left the building, he felt a glimmer of hope that something might come from the meeting. He'd been writing new songs and working with a few musicians he had met through adverts he'd placed in the national music papers, but he knew they weren't quite there yet. He needed something to push him over the edge and give him that extra spark.

It had been nearly ten months since he'd left The Innocent, four months since he'd had the argument with Alicia that had put an end to whatever it was that they'd shared. It was funny but he didn't miss her at all, he was totally focused on himself now.

A few weeks later, Billy's new band had managed to secure a gig at a small venue in Wembley. Billy had invited Barry to come and watch them play, hoping to impress him enough to secure a record deal. His band had put on a good performance, even if there weren't many people in attendance. It was nothing like what he'd experienced when he played with Vince and the others. As he left the stage, he saw Barry standing at the bar. He decided to go over and talk to him.

"It's not what I'm looking for," Barry had said before turning his back and returning to his conversation with two of his friends. Billy felt his heart sink. He had given it his all and it still wasn't enough. He shook his head sadly and walked away.

The days and weeks that followed were hard for Billy, he questioned his music and wondered if he was really good enough to make it or whether he should just give up now before things got any worse. His confidence had taken a major blow, especially after the rejection from Barry Marlow.

With no clear direction in sight, Billy thought long and hard about what to do next. He started to doubt himself and his ability as a singer-songwriter. He thought back to the night of the gig again in his head, he went over and over their performance trying to think how it could have been better but still came up with nothing, maybe Barry was right, maybe he wasn't talented enough musically to make it in the music business.

The following Friday afternoon Billy was strolling along Wardour Street when he noticed a familiar figure walking towards him. They got close and the figure immediately looked up, grinning from ear to ear.

"Hey there! How have you been?" Vince said as he hugged Billy. "So I assume all the bad stuff is forgotten then?" Billy replied, his voice muffled in Vince's embrace. "Of course it is," Vince smiled, "life's too short to be fighting with people who matter to you." Billy was delighted to hear these words; he'd missed being in The Innocent so much. "Do you want to get a drink?" Vince gestured with his head towards The Ship on the other side of the road. "Why not?" Billy answered, "you can tell me what's been happening for the past ten months."

They walked over to The Ship and ordered a couple of beers, before Vince started talking. He told Billy about how he'd been playing gigs in different clubs around London. He also mentioned that Paul and Micky had left the band and had decided to do their own thing, they'd both gone back to Birmingham, as without a deal of any sort they'd run short of money. Vince had replaced them with a drummer called Steve and a bass player who called himself Johnny.

Billy couldn't believe what he was hearing, it seemed like his dream of being part of The Innocent again was over now that both Paul and Micky were gone. He felt a wave of disappointment as Vince continued, "You know," he said looking directly at Billy, "you're the only one who could truly revive the sound I'm trying to recreate with The Innocent."

Billy looked up in surprise, unsure if he'd heard correctly. Was Vince really asking for his help after all this time? Everything Vince said next confirmed it; he was asking Billy to join the band again! He thanked Vince but asked why he needed him when there were clearly plenty of talented musicians out there who could take his place.

"Because no one can do what you do," Vince replied without hesitation. "You have a unique musical ability, we work well together, your song writing is brilliant, and your voice is pure magic!"

Billy blushed at these compliments, never before had anyone praised him so highly about his work or talent, it felt incredible! Without hesitation, Billy accepted the offer and got up to fetch some more drinks by way of celebration. When they'd talked for what seemed like hours, he decided to go home and start writing some new songs for The Innocent's revival!

As Billy walked through the busy streets of London, his mind was racing with new ideas. He couldn't wait to get back into the studio with Vince and start creating music again. He knew that they could make something truly special together.

The days that followed were a blur of activity for Billy. He spent most of his time writing new songs and rehearsing with Vince and the two new guys, getting ready for their first gig together in nearly a year. The day of the gig arrived and Billy was nervous but also excited to be playing with Vince again.

After the show, Vince called Billy over to the side of the stage. "That was amazing," he said, putting his hand on Billy's shoulder. "I can't believe I ever let you go." Billy smiled, feeling overcome with emotion. "I'm just glad to be back," he replied.

The turnout for the gig had been alright, but it was clear that they needed to do more if they wanted to make a proper comeback. With this in mind, Vince and Billy decided to plan a small tour. It wasn't as successful as they had hoped; there were some venues with barely more than a dozen people in attendance. Discouraged by their lack of success, Vince thought the band should make one final attempt at finding a manager who could help them succeed. He had contacted someone who had been responsible for the success of a rock band from Finland, this man had moulded the band from the beginning of their careers and guided them through the early stages of touring and recording, and now, they were gaining global recognition. The two of them made plans for The Innocent to fly to Finland and perform at the Tavastia Club in Helsinki.

The cool breeze of early morning nibbled at Billy's cheeks and nose and stung his half-closed eyes. The sun had not yet cleared the horizon, but it would soon. He inhaled deep breaths of the crystal clear Scandinavian air as he strolled across the tarmac and into the terminal, taking in the myriad of new sights and sounds that he'd never experienced before. The plane had landed with a heavy thud like an angry bull, its brakes had roared into life to slow it down and then taxied down a nearby runway, sending a shock wave large enough to rock Billy back into his seat. As the band gathered their bags from the baggage claim and exited the terminal they were nearly run over by two tall men in black suits who were arguing about which direction to go in. They made their way out to get a taxi to take them to their hotel. The driver spoke no English, but there was a universal language for communication, money. They climbed into the backseat of the cab and headed into town. Tonight they would play at The Tavastia Club for Antti Nieminen, the manager Vince had been communicating with. It was their first visit to Helsinki, and they hoped that this trip could launch their career forwards again. Twelve months ago Someday Remember had reached the top ten in Finland's music charts. This was going to be much more than a one off show; it was a chance at legitimacy.

The stage was in shadow as the intro music played. A single note hung suspended in the heavy air, like a weight separating heaven and hell, then crashed down on Billy's guitar. Vince cried out with sharp, clear vocals, while Johnny ripened their sound with a thick bass groove and Steve beat out a rhythm on his drums. Against a dimmed backdrop of dark velvet curtains, they thundered into the first song. The walls shook, the crowd roared, the band was back!

The gig went as planned, but it wasn't the same without Micky and Paul. Billy could hear something different in the sound, but he and Vince carried on regardless with drive and passion, treating the show like a love letter to their past members. Billy looked out into the crowd, memories flashing back to other gigs they'd played. The faces were different, the energy felt the same but the special bond on stage wasn't there.

As the performance ended, cheers rang out and people clapped but there was no encore! After saying goodbye to their fans, they all headed backstage to discuss their next steps.

Vince is acting out of character thought Billy, as he observed his friend getting ready to meet Annti Nieminen. Vince had performed spectacularly onstage, appearing in control and exuding confidence, taking command of the entire space like it was his due. But now he seemed a bit uncomfortable. Vince hadn't taken part in any of the rider they'd been given before the show, nothing afterwards either, no drugs, no women, nothing. He glanced at Billy and simply said he was going to see Annti, "wish me luck," he smiled as he exited the room.

Billy sat in silence as he waited for Vince to return, Steve and Johnny had gone out to join in with the crowd but Billy wanted to hear what Vince had to say, it had been about half an hour now so hopefully everything was going according to plan.

Twenty minutes later Billy looked up to see Vince standing in the doorway to the dressing room, he had a smile on his face and Billy took this to mean that the meeting had gone well.

Billy's face lit up in anticipation when he asked Vince, "What did he say? Is he going to manage us?"

Vince sighed and shook his head. "He didn't speak. When I walked up to him, I could see he was surrounded by a group of rowdy friends at a big round table in the

VIP section. He looked up at me, paused for a moment as if trying to remember something, then smiled drunkenly and slowly slipped off his chair under the table. I'm pretty sure he had no idea who we were or what we sounded like. This whole thing has been a total waste of time and money."

Billy's heart sank. They had flown all the way to Helsinki for nothing? He couldn't believe it. He had never seen Vince so defeated before. He looked at his friend, trying to think of something to say to lift his spirits. "We can't give up now," he said, placing a reassuring hand on Vince's shoulder. "We've come too far to let this beat us. We'll keep pushing and working harder until we get to where we want to be." Vince gave him a small smile, "Let's just go and get pissed!" he said as he got up, "there's nothing we can do about it now and we're here till tomorrow night so we may as well enjoy ourselves come on, let's get out there."

The rest of the night passed in a blur. Billy couldn't even remember what they had done or where they had gone.

As they sat in the airport bar waiting to board the plane back to London, Billy felt the disappointment weighing heavily on him. But he refused to give up. He knew that he and Vince had something special and they just needed to find the right person to help them get their music out there.

"Things will get better," he muttered to himself. "They have to."

"I'll get us another drink," Vince's words broke his thought pattern, "you want the same again?"

"Yes please mate," Billy replied looking up, "get us a couple of chasers as well though, we may as well enjoy something about this trip before we start again when we get home."

Vince collected up the empty glasses that seemed to be multiplying on their table and made his way to the bar, returning ten minutes later with a tray full of drinks. "I got us two rounds," he said as he set the tray on the table, "It seems a bit pointless to keep getting up to get more."

The two friends spent the next two hours in high spirits drinking and laughing, reminiscing about their trip to Finland. When the final call came for their flight back to London they both looked at each other and said, "Shall we have another drink? We can take the next plane."

Five hours later they made their way to the check-in desk looking to get on the flight to Heathrow that had just been announced. "May I see your tickets and passport, please?" A polite lady wearing a wide smile and a blue uniform asked them when it was their turn. Vince handed her the tickets and they both gave her their passports, but as soon as she saw them her smile faded away. She explained that the tickets were for the previous flight and that they would need to buy new ones for the next available one, this flight was already full so she couldn't help them.

"Why can't we get on this one?" Billy slurred through his alcohol-induced haze. "We've paid for these tickets."

"You have to take the flight that the tickets are allocated for," she replied somewhat impatiently, like she was having to explain basic flying principles to two drunken idiots. "The tickets aren't transferable, I'm sorry but I can't help you. You'll need to go over there to the help desk and see what can be done," she pointed out where they needed to go behind them and the two of them walked over.

"The lady says we can't board this plane," Billy slurred as another woman in a matching uniform asked if she could help them, "can we get the next one?" "Yes of course," the woman replied, her smile beaming, "It departs at 07.27 tomorrow morning, how would you like to pay?" The two of them looked at each, their faces full of resignation, "we'll be back in a minute," Billy slurred, then the two of them slowly made their way to the exit.

Chapter Thirty-One

B illy and Vince strolled through the Senate Square, admiring the iconic Helsinki cathedral. They stopped to take in the view of the harbour front, with its vibrant cafes, shops and outdoor food stalls. After arriving via taxi from the airport, they were trying to decide what their next steps should be.

"What do we do now?" Billy asked as he sat down on a bench, resting his feet on his bag. Vince was lost in thought and didn't respond immediately. "I don't have enough for another plane ticket," he finally muttered.

"Me neither," Billy said glumly, "We need to find somewhere to stay tonight but getting a hotel will clean us out completely." Suddenly, Vince's face lit up with an idea.

"Do you remember those sisters we met at Studio Valbonne back in London?" Billy looked at him blankly.

Vince continued, "Oh wait, it wasn't you, it was Paul

and Micky who were there. But anyway, these girls were called Kristiina and Kerttu."

"How can I remember someone I've never met before?" Billy interrupted, clearly confused by Vince's ramblings.

"They were at The Tavastia, we were speaking to them, don't you remember?"

Billy had been so out of it at The Tavastia after the disappointment of not getting a new manager that he couldn't remember anything about the night.

"Anyway, it doesn't matter. They live here in Helsinki, maybe they can help us out with a place to stay?"

"How can we ask complete strangers for help?" Billy questioned sceptically.

Vince kept talking, "Kerttu and I aren't total strangers, she gave me her number and said if we wanted to meet before we leave then we should give her a ring."

Billy's mood lightened slightly at the thought of having some help. "So why don't you phone her?", he suggested.

"Let's find a phone," Vince spoke as he was looking around, "There, lets go to that cafe and I'll give her a call."

Billy followed Vince to the cafe where he sat down at a small table as Vince went to use the payphone hanging on the wall just behind him. Billy could hear the faint sound of the phone ringing on the other end before it was picked up.

"Hello?" he heard a voice say on the other end.

"Hey, Kerttu, it's Vince. Do you remember me?" Vince asked.

"Oh, hi Vince! Of course I remember you. How's Helsinki treating you?"

"It's been a bit of a tough one, actually. We missed our flight and we don't have a place to stay. Do you think you could help us out?" Vince asked, hoping against hope that she would say yes.

"Of course! Jaakko and I have a spare bed in our apartment. You're more than welcome to stay with us," Kerttu said, her voice full of warmth and friendliness.

Vince turned to Billy with a smile of triumph on his face. "We have a place to stay!"

Billy couldn't believe it. They had come all this way, only to be faced with failure at every turn, and yet somehow, things always seemed to work out for them. He couldn't help feeling grateful for Vince's resourcefulness.

"Thank you so much, Kerttu. You have no idea how much this means to us," Vince said, full of gratitude.

"It's no problem at all. We're happy to help," Kerttu replied. "Do you need me to give you directions to our apartment?"

Vince nodded eagerly as he said yes, and Kerttu gave him the address along with detailed instructions on how to get there.

They made their way to the bus stop in the corner of the square and followed Kerttu's instructions until they reached a five-storey set of apartment blocks. She was waving at them from the balcony on the first floor, telling them to press the bell so she could let them in. When they stepped through her doorway, there was a tall young man about twenty-five years old waiting for them.

"This is Jaakko," Kerttu said with a smile as she introduced him, "my boyfriend." They all exchanged friendly handshakes before Billy and Vince settled into the large brown sofa while Jaakko got them each a beer from the fridge. The living room was bright and inviting, with a small kitchen-diner tucked into one corner. A few steps away, there was a bathroom with just enough space to manoeuvre around. But it was the bed that caught their attention, high up above the television area, supported by a sturdy double frame and accessed by a metal ladder. They smiled in unison; this would be perfect for their short stay.

They stayed for four nights and Vince and Billy were treated with nothing but kindness and hospitality. Jaakko and Kerttu welcomed them into their home, even offering to take them around and show them the city. Kerttu's sister Kristiina, came over one night and she and Vince went out to spend some time together. On Sunday night, Kerttu cooked up a hearty meal of reindeer stew with mashed potatoes, before sharing a bottle of Finnish blackberry wine as they sat around the kitchen table. The next morning they said their goodbyes, both Vince and Billy thanked their hosts for their warmth and generosity.

The pair could only hope that one day they would be able to repay the kindness they had received from this special couple that had opened up their home so willingly in a moment of need.

The two friends made their way back to the heart of Helsinki in search of a way home to London. At a travel agency, they were informed that the best course of action would be to take a ferry from Helsinki to Stockholm, then catch a train to Gothenburg and board another ferry to Frederikshavn in Denmark, where they could find trains leading them back into France. After deciding on this plan, the two of them left the shop and started their walk towards the harbour to board a ferry.

When they arrived at the harbour, it was too late to get on a ferry for that day. The next available ticket was for the following evening and so they bought two. Now they needed something to do and somewhere to sleep that night. Vince tried phoning Kerttu again to ask if they could go back there, but he couldn't get an answer. So, they chose to go to a bar for a while to keep warm, but eventually decided that going back to the apartment was their best option, they would ask if they could stay for one last night.

When they arrived, the place was deserted and the temperature seemed to be dropping. Vince looked up at the balcony and remembered that it wasn't always locked; he suggested they should climb up there while they waited for their friends to get back. Billy stood on Vince's shoulders and climbed up onto the balcony before catching the bags that Vince threw up to him. The plan was for Billy to hang a strap off one of their bags down so Vince could use it to get himself onto the balcony. Vince tucked a bottle of vodka that they had bought for their journey home into his jumper so he could use both hands to climb, it fell through and smashed on the floor, he hadn't tucked his top into his trousers!

"Fucking hell," Billy said, sounding really annoyed. They wouldn't have anything to drink to help keep them warm until they returned home now. "How am I going to get up there?" Vince asked as it became clear that getting him up was not going to be easy. He tried various ways to climb up but after struggling for ten minutes declared that he was going to look for a warm place and left, leaving Billy alone on the balcony.

Billy wondered how long Kerttu and Jaakko would be gone, the door was locked and the air had become increasingly chilly. He lay down and used his bag as a pillow. He was shaken awake by Jaakko telling him to get inside where it was warm. It was one o'clock in the morning, and Billy had been outside for almost four hours.

Bright and early the next morning, a frantic ringing of the doorbell shook Billy awake. It was Vince, with a flustered expression on his face.

Over breakfast and coffee at the kitchen table, he began to tell them about his evening. He had found a bar near one of the apartment blocks and gone in to keep warm. To Vince's surprise, a man and his wife had recognised him as the lead singer from The Innocent, seemingly remembering him from the Travastia gig. They welcomed him into their group and bought him drinks all night before offering him a bed in their home. Vince couldn't recall the husband's name, but he remembered that this man had given him a guitar and requested that he play, unfortunately he only knew one song on the guitar.

Apparently, Vince had sung "House of the Rising Sun." over twenty times before finally being allowed to stop. When he awoke that morning, he was in bed with the wife while four young children stared at him from the foot of the bed. With no memory of how he had got there or what was in his drinks (which appeared to be vodka but very strong), Vince quickly dressed and ran back to their apartment. Laughter filled the air as everyone agreed that it was probably time for them to leave Finland and take a ferry home.

The ferry was an overnight trip and Billy and Vince found themselves in the disco on the top deck. A few older women danced together, drinking and laughing, talking about who knows what. Everyone seemed to have someone with them except for two business men who sat at the bar in their suits, reading their papers and drinking their drinks like strangers. Within an hour it was just the two of them and Vince was hopping around trying to get some money out of his boot to buy another drink. It had been put there to stop them wasting money unnecessarily.

The barman told them they could have one more drink each before he had to close up for the night, and that it was time for them to go back to their cabins. However, they had chosen the cheapest tickets available which didn't include a cabin, so the two of them settled down on a single seat each outside one of the restaurants trying to get as comfortable they could.

By morning, the ferry was sailing into Stockholm's harbour and with bleary eyes, they gathered together their things and disembarked onto the dockside searching for directions to the train station. As they sat on the train through Sweden towards Gothenburg, all they could see were miles upon miles of dense green pine trees. It wasn't very exciting scenery.

They arrived in Gothenburg and made their way down to the port for a ferry, they were told it would be five hours so they found themselves a cafe and sat there for the whole time nursing one drink each, Billy couldn't believe how expensive it had been for just two drinks and the two of them vowed that this one would last them the whole five hours.

When they arrived in Denmark they started to feel a little bit more energetic, but it was still a long journey home. They ended up walking for three days and two nights, jumping on trains when possible and having to hide away from the ticket inspectors whenever trains stopped at stations. On the third night as they crept onto another train without tickets, the German conductor had not understood them when they tried to explain that they weren't able to purchase tickets and someone would meet them in Cologne to pay for them. He shook his head and moved down the carriage, leaving the two of them thinking that they had seemingly managed to sneak a free ride. When the train stopped in Dusseldorf, a large inspector got on and addressed them fluently in English. She asked for their tickets, which they were unable to provide. Feeling like there was nothing else they could do, Billy and Vince left the train and found themselves freezing cold and extremely hungry in the middle of old town Dusseldorf. The last food the pair had bought had been a sweet spread, or so they thought, from a shop in southern Denmark, but it turned out to be a cold toast topper instead, this had made their only snack in three days, one slice of bread covered with this mystery spread, even less appealing. The locals around them enjoyed the vibrant bars and restaurants, whilst the two of them regretfully sat in silence wishing they had got on the plane when they'd heard the final call.

Vince urged Billy to follow him and the two of them searched for somewhere safe to sleep, they discovered a clearing below a bridge that crossed the river Rhine.

Exhausted, they simply curled up in the freezing cold. Hugging each other tightly for warmth, they braced themselves for an uncomfortable evening ahead. After what seemed like an eternity lying awake in the cold night air, they finally decided to approach the Dusseldorf police station and ask for help finding their way home.

The two of them had been in the police station for over eight hours, where they were given food, drinks, and tickets back to Dover. They weren't sure how it had happened, but the German police had communicated with the British Embassy who had managed to arrange their passage back home. Now, they were on a train bound for Ostend in Belgium, from where they would board a ferry and eventually make it back to England. They didn't question their luck; they just felt relieved to have the journey home underway.

When they reached Dover, Billy called his father Alastair, begging him to purchase two tickets on his credit card so that they could travel back to London. Begrudgingly, he agreed. As they got off the train at Waterloo station, they had to frantically jump over the ticket barriers in order to catch a tube. The same thing happened again when they reached Clapham North, they didn't even have enough money for the tube fare. After finally making it back to Billy's flat, he phoned his father once more, letting him know that they were safe. With that, they both settled down in the warmth and comfort of Billy's flat, sleep came easily for them.

Chapter Thirty-Two

I t had been nearly three months since The Innocent had returned from Finland and Vince and Billy's efforts to secure a record deal or financial backing hadn't borne fruit. The two of them had decided to make the trip to Toronto to find out the truth about the Earthlines deal Lennie Ratcliffe had offered them, only to discover the company was in fact bankrupt and the building they visited had obviously been abandoned.

They stayed with Vince's uncle and his family, Vince's cousin Terry, took them out on a tour of local attractions and live music venues. They even got up onstage to play a handful of songs with one band, which were received well by the enthusiastic audience but that was as close as they got to a live performance.

Unfortunately, their journey to New York on a Greyhound bus proved equally unfruitful. Despite their hopes of setting up some meetings with record labels whilst in New York, nothing came of it. When he witnessed the level of guitar playing from all the bands that seemed to be playing in every bar or club they walked past, Billy realised just how much work he had to do to keep up with those musicians.

Once they'd made their way back to London, the two of them played some gigs in an effort to rekindle old interests, but to no avail and soon enough, Billy and Vince were growing apart. They'd still meet up occasionally for a night on the town or a few drinks, but when Vince told him that he was quitting the band and jetting off to Spain with his girlfriend, it didn't shock Billy. She had some friends she wanted him to meet in Zaragoza so he thought it would be fun to start again in a different place.

The night before he left, Billy and Vince met up in Soho for one last hurrah. As they had so many times before, the two enjoyed a wild night out. When it was time to part ways, they shared an embrace and wished each other well, knowing that their paths would cross again in the future, they had developed a special bond. As Billy returned home later that night, he couldn't help but shed a few tears; it felt like the end of an era. Unable to sleep, he lay awake with his mind spinning with ideas. He knew the next day presented another opportunity, one that he was determined to grasp.

Billy woke up bright and early; he got himself ready and took the train to north London. After getting off at

Finsbury Park station, he walked along Seven Sisters Road before winding his way through some back streets. Finally, he stumbled across the cafe where he'd agreed to meet the drummer who'd been in the band he'd formed when he'd left The Innocent. As soon as he opened the door, John stood up from his table surrounded by four others and welcomed him with a friendly smile. The cafe was small but cosy, with wooden flooring and a few vintage posters on the wall. Billy sat down as John introduced him to the others, a bassist, a rhythm guitarist, a keyboardist and John's wife Carla. They exchanged pleasantries before getting down to business, discussing their future as a band.

Over the next few hours, they talked about their musical influences and shared some of their work with each other. Billy was impressed with their talent and enthusiasm and they agreed to meet up the following week to rehearse.

As Billy walked back to the train station, he felt energised and excited for the first time in a long while. He knew that this was the start of something new and that he was finally going to make it as a musician. As he passed by a record shop, he recalled his father's words, "dreaming about the big time won't get you anywhere unless you put in the hard work!" Billy was determined to do just that.

Over the next few weeks, he spent every moment he could rehearsing with his new band mates, and they soon had a solid set of songs. They started playing small gigs in local pubs and bars but Billy's heart wasn't really in it.

The other members of the band were heavy drinkers and cannabis smokers, even before they went on stage. This lack of commitment affected him and he knew he was losing interest. He also started drinking and smoking heavily along with them. Rather than going to West End clubs like he used to, he was now spending most of his time in basement rooms or dirty apartments. The champagne and cocaine had been replaced by cheap lager and speed that he took by wrapping it in a single sheet of toilet paper and swallowing it. One weekend, Billy spent the entire time vomiting thick green bile as a result of taking a bad wrap of speed one night. He felt like he was on a downward spiral and there seemed to be no escape.

Billy awoke to a sound of someone pounding on his flat door. As he came round from another night of alcohol and drugs, he got up and scrambled to answer it. When the door opened, a scowling landlord and one of his sons were standing there. The son held a folded piece of paper in his hand and motioned for Billy to follow him. "You need to come with us to the post office," the landlord said sternly in his thick French accent, "you're behind on the rent again and I want you to cash this cheque and give me the money, then I want you to leave the flat by the end of next week."

Billy's heart sank as he looked at the DHSS rent cheque that was sent to him each month. He had cashed them in but spent the money elsewhere, on drinks and cigarettes mostly, it explained why he hadn't managed to pay the rent for two months now. "That's my personal post," he snarled as realisation struck him, "you can't just take it and open it whenever you feel like it."

"I've taken it because you couldn't be trusted with it," his landlord replied. His tone indicated he was finished discussing the matter: "Now, get dressed and come with us."

Billy shut the door as he got ready, knowing that his careless spending habits were finally catching up with him.

He found himself in the back of his landlord's car, with two other men on either side of him and the son in front. "This is all a bit dramatic isn't it?" he said sarcastically as they all stared at him and the son in the front seat flashed some sort of identification, "what are you going to do with that?" He asked as he motioned towards it, "Is that your membership to twat's are us?" The son put down his hand and smiled menacingly and the landlord started the car and drove off.

Ten minutes later Billy was standing at the counter in the main post office on Clapham High Road as the cashier asked him how he'd like his money.

"It doesn't matter thank you, I'm only going to give it to Rigsby here," he said as he nodded his head in the direction of the man standing next to him. The cashier smiled up at him, clearly amused by the reference to his landlord. She counted out the money and passed it to him. "There you go," she said with a friendly smile, "enjoy the rest of your day now."

"Thanks a lot," Billy responded with a nod as he collected his money and walked away from the counter. When they reached the pavement outside Billy passed the notes to his landlord who was standing far too close for comfort. "Here," he said as he handed back a five pound note, "make sure to have your things out of my flat by Friday."

Billy was waiting by Elephant and Castle tube station when Jimmy's car, a battered blue ford escort, pulled up. Jimmy waved Billy over, he got in and they drove away from all the hustle and bustle near the dingy station.

Billy had asked if Jimmy knew anyone willing to loan him some money. In three days time, he'd have to leave his flat but needed a deposit for another place. Plus, if he could get some cash together, he could hire a top producer so that his new band could go into the studio and record some high quality music. He thought that doing this would allow him to take their recordings around to different labels and get a record deal, solving all his problems. Jimmy said there were people he knew who might lend Billy the funds he needed and they were now on their way to meet them.

They pulled into the car park of The Black Flag and made their way inside, Jimmy leading the way. The bar was dimly lit and smoky, with the sound of loud music filling the air. They bought drinks and made their way to a booth in the corner.

"I might know someone who can help you out, but they'll want something in return," Jimmy said, his eyes flickering over to Billy.

Billy shifted uncomfortably in his seat, an uneasy feeling creeping up his spine. He had a bad feeling about where this was heading.

"What do you mean?" he asked cautiously. Jimmy leaned in closer, his face serious. "The guy I know will give you the money, but if you don't pay him back on time, he'll come after you," He warned him in a low voice.

Billy nodded, unsure of what to do, everything had seemed so clear back in his flat when he was sitting with a vodka and coke in his hand, but now that he was here, in this dusky bar filled with smoke and danger, doubt had started to creep in.

He glanced towards the back of the room, where a giant man wearing a leather jacket stood talking with a scruffy middle-aged man who had two huge shaven headed figures flanking him. Tears glided down his face as he asked something of the man in the leather jacket who grabbed hold of his shoulders and squeezed tight. After a few moments, the middle-aged man ran away looking much more relieved. The man in the leather jacket grinned malevolently.

Jimmy quietly asked, "Are you sure you want to get mixed up with this kind of crowd?" He could tell that Billy was having second thoughts as he was slowly realising the full extent of what he was getting himself into.

"Once you take anything from them, they'll have a hold on you," Jimmy continued, "they won't ever let you go and they'll be part of your life forever. Is that really what you want?"

"Then why'd you bring me here in the first place?" asked Billy. "If it's not a good idea, why did we even bother coming?"

Jimmy smiled before answering, "You wouldn't have believed me if I just told you about these people. I know how stubborn you are, you always think that you can do whatever you want. I'm just trying to warn you that it won't end too well for you. I wanted to show you so that you can make a better informed decision before making any commitments."

Billy leaned back in his chair and sighed heavily, he definitely didn't want to be associated with something like this. He looked at Jimmy gratefully and said, "Thanks for bringing me here first, mate. You might have just saved me from making a mistake I'd regret forever." Jimmy put his hand on Billy's arm in a friendly way and reassured him that it was no problem, and then the two of them finished their drinks and left.

CHAPTER THIRTY-THREE

Billy climbed onto the number 242 bus, feeling a little overwhelmed by his belongings. A heavy guitar case in one hand, a black holdall straining at its seams hung from one shoulder and his rucksack was slung over the opposite side. He had stuffed three large black bin bags with all his worldly possessions, and struggled to hold everything whilst he found just enough coins to pay for his ticket.

The journey seemed to take forever as he made his way from Bethnal Green tube station to Dalston, where Nick, the keyboard player in his new band, lived in a one-bedroom flat on the third floor of a crumbling council estate. Nick had offered Billy a place to stay until he could find somewhere more permanent.

As the bus finally pulled up to his stop, Billy's stomach sank. He had been dreading this moment for a while, but there was no turning back now. Collecting his bags, he carefully navigated his way through the bustling streets towards the estate. His heart raced as he laid eyes on the towering block of dingy brown bricks, six storeys high with grimy wet staircases at each end.

Taking a deep breath, he stepped into one of the stairwells and was immediately hit by a smell of urine and the sight of broken needles littering the floor. He trudged up the steps until he arrived on the third floor and made his way along the concrete walkway, stepping over rubbish bags and rusty bikes until he reached Nick's front door.

He reluctantly knocked and waited for an answer, Nick gave Billy a warm smile as he unlocked the door and gestured for him to step inside. He was met with a smell he couldn't quite put his finger on. It wasn't exactly unpleasant, just unfamiliar. The flat was small and cluttered, with a few musical instruments scattered around the room. Billy couldn't help but notice the makeshift recording studio set up in the corner of Nick's bedroom, complete with a couple of microphones and a tape deck. Nick had put a double mattress on the floor in one corner of the living room with a couple of pillows, an off white sheet and a dark brown eiderdown cover. Billy threw his bags onto the bed and let out a sigh of relief.

"So," Nick said as he sat down on the sofa, "how was your day?"

Billy shook his head and collapsed onto the mattress

next to his bags. "It was rough," he said with a sigh. "Feels like everything's falling apart."

Nick nodded sympathetically. "I know how you feel," he said. "Starting a new band is never easy, especially when you're broke, and it's even worse when you've got to think about finding somewhere to live."

Billy nodded and sighed. "I just wish things were easier, you know?" he said. "I wish I didn't have to worry about money all the time, I just want to be able to focus on my music and see if I can make something from it."

Nick smiled softly and put his hand on Billy's shoulder. "I know," he said. "But things will get better. We just have to keep working at it."

Billy nodded and lay back on the bed. He closed his eyes and took a deep breath, trying to clear his mind of all the stress that had been plaguing him. For a moment, he forgot about the dingy flat and the uncertainty of his future. He tried to imagine himself on stage, the bright lights illuminating his face, his guitar in his hands, and the sound of the crowd cheering him on. It was a distant dream, but it was what kept him going.

As he opened his eyes, he noticed something strange in the corner of the room. At first, he thought it was just a trick of the light, but then he saw it move again. It was a mouse, scurrying along the floorboards, its beady eyes fixed on Billy. He scrambled up from the bed, his heart racing as he watched the rodent disappear into a crack in the wall. Nick noticed the look of disgust on Billy's face and chuckled. "Yeah, we get a few of them around here," he said. "But you get used to them after a while."

Billy shook his head, unable to shake the image of the mouse out of his mind. As much as he tried to rationalise the situation, he couldn't help but feel like he was in over his head. He had left everything he knew behind, and now he was living in a rundown flat, surrounded by strangers and mice. It was a far cry from the life he had imagined for himself, but he had no other choice.

He looked over at Nick, who seemed unfazed by the situation. He was busy tinkering with one of his keyboards, lost in thought.

Billy sighed and got to his feet. "I'm going out," he said. "I need to get some air."

Nick nodded, barely looking up from the keyboard. "Alright," he said. "Just watch yourself out there, okay? Dalston can be a rough place at night."

Billy nodded and grabbed his jacket from the bed before heading out into the night. He hadn't been in Dalston for long, but he had already heard horror stories about it, fights breaking out in the streets and people getting mugged. He tried not to let these stories affect him, though he could feel an uneasiness growing inside of him as he made his way through the winding alley-ways. He wondered what had made him want to go for a walk on his own and decided that it had been a stupid idea.

He kept his head down and focused on getting back

home, but soon enough something caught his eye, a group of black men standing near a side door that led into an alleyway behind one of the buildings. They were all wearing dark clothing and were speaking in hushed tones, but Billy could sense by their demeanour that they were up to no good. As soon as they saw him approaching them, one of them stepped forward and gestured for him to stop walking. Billy froze in fear as the guy glared at him menacingly with cold eyes that seemed to hold a thousand secrets within them.

Billy looked around for help but there was nobody else around except for this small group of thugs who seemed completely unperturbed by his presence. His instinct to run kicked in and without further hesitation he bolted, running away as fast as he could the way he had come, his heart pounding in his chest as he desperately tried to make it back to Nick's flat.

After what felt like an eternity, he made it back safe and sound, his shirt soaked with sweat and his breathing heavy. He was relieved to be back but the experience had shaken him up. He stepped inside and closed the door behind him, locking out the darkness of the night.

The weeks and months dragged on, with the band only able to afford one rehearsal a week. In the meantime, Nick and Billy would sometimes practise together in their flat, although Nick usually lit up when he did, due to his penchant for smoking marijuana. Billy felt stifled by the constant lingering smell of the drug surrounding him in the flat but was too nervous to go out alone after dark due to his traumatic first night in the area.

His stomach grumbled as he sustained himself on cheap cans of beans and soups from the corner shop, though if he were lucky enough he could scavenge some more substantial items from shoplifting. He'd stuff blocks of cheese into his jacket sleeve or cold slices of ham into his shirt, occasionally managing to smuggle out ready-made meals if he got lucky and picked the right shop with an easily distracted assistant.

It wasn't a sustainable way of living, but it was all he had at the moment. His dream of making it as a musician felt like it was slipping further away with each passing day, and he couldn't help but feel like he was drowning. He tried to stay positive, but it was hard when he was constantly reminded of his situation. The flat was cold and damp, and the sound of the mice scurrying along the floorboards at night kept him awake.

Billy felt like he had reached his lowest point when he was forced to sign on the dole. He had searched for a part time job in the area but nothing suitable was available. He trudged back to the flat but as he stepped inside, something unexpected greeted him. Nick was with John's wife Carla, the two of them lying together in bed half naked.

They didn't notice that he had just walked in, too busy giggling and grabbing at each other with wild abandon. It was clear from their faces that they had both been drinking heavily, although neither of them seemed to notice what was going on around them, oblivious to Billy standing there in shock. They finally noticed him when they heard him gasp in surprise as he surveyed the scene before him. Angry and confused, all he could do was step out of the room unable to process what had just happened.

Ten minutes later, the two of them were standing in the living room.

"Are you fucking kidding me?" Billy shouted. "You're married to his best friend. What's wrong with you? How could you do that?"

"We love each other," Carla answered softly. "We wanted to be together, but it's a difficult situation."

"Fucking difficult situation?" Billy retorted, not believing what he was hearing. "I can't fucking believe this! How am I supposed to look John in the eye and pretend I don't know anything about it? Just as the band was starting to really get somewhere, you two go and fucking ruin it all. You selfish bitch! How could you?"

Carla's face fell and she stood there silently, not knowing what to say in response. Nick started to say something but thought better of it, then he looked at Billy and said, "I think you'd better move out mate." It was then that Billy realised that his dream was over. He silently walked over to his bed and curled up into a ball as his eyes filled with angry tears.

The next morning he was up early, and as he passed the full-length mirror on the way to the bathroom, he was shocked by what he saw. The thin material of his boxers hung over the bones of his hips and across the bottom of a bloated stomach. His eyes were sunken and rheumy, his hair was matted with sweat and grease, and his chin was covered with two days' growth. He couldn't believe that this was the same person who had only eighteen months ago been in a successful band playing to thousands of people with a song in the charts. He looked at himself in disgust.

He dressed and made his way outside; he walked down the stinking stairway out onto the cold concrete expanse of the estate. He walked towards the shop and picked up the receiver of the payphone in the red telephone box that stood outside.

"I need to come home mum," he said sadly when Pauline answered.

CHAPTER THIRTY-FOUR

Billy stepped off the Midland Red bus from Birmingham as it pulled up in the bus station of his hometown. He'd set out from London on a National Express coach earlier that day and now here he was, hobbling across the road carrying his guitar and the pathetic array of meagre possessions he'd managed to bring with him.

His mother Pauline was standing across the road leaning against her white Morris Marina, her face immediately registering shock at the state of her son.

"Hello love," she said gently.

"Hello mum," he quietly responded, lowering his head in shame.

Pauline saw the devastation in her son's face and immediately understood that he was broken. She quickly ushered him into the car, not wanting to draw any attention from passers-by.

As they drove away, Pauline glanced at Billy and, without asking any questions about what had happened, offered a silent assurance that everything would be alright.

When they arrived home she put her arm around him and said, "Come on then, let's get you something to eat." She made him some of his favourite food, then sat with him while he ate it in silence. Afterwards she took him upstairs and laid out some fresh sheets on the bed in his old room.

As they stood there Pauline looked at Billy again and asked softly, "Do you need anything else love?" He shook his head then Pauline added gently, "Get yourself in the shower and then get some rest."

Billy did as he was told, and as the warm water ran over his body he felt all of the dirt and grime from the past months wash away and he finally started to cry.

The tears flowed for a long time, then he stepped out of the shower and into some clean clothes, for the first time in ages, he felt the comfort of being in familiar surroundings. He joined his mum in the living room comforted by the thought that he was home and away from the chaos of the past few years.

Pauline made him a cup of tea and they talked long into the night about his time in London and all the mistakes he had made.

At the end of it all, Pauline put her arm around her son, pulled him close and told him, "It's going to be alright love, you just have to keep going no matter how tough it gets."

Billy nodded, a little bit of hope beginning to blossom in his heart, and he realised then that even in the darkest of moments, you can still find a glimmer of light.

The following morning, Billy Maguire sat at the dining table in his parent's house tucking into some toast and marmalade with a cup of steaming hot tea.

"Hello son," beamed his father in a thick Scottish accent, "how was the big time?"

Acknowledgments

This book was born from a deep desire to share Billy's story - a tale that has been brewing within me for some time.

Although Someday Remember is a work of fiction, the character of Billy Maguire is one that I feel deeply connected to, as his journey through music and life echoes many of my own experiences.

I would like to express my gratitude to Lee Mark Jones, Nigel Kirwan, and John Lahiffe for their friendship, memories, and inspiration in shaping some of the characters in this book. In my life, I have encountered a diverse array of individuals who possess unique qualities and traits that can also be seen reflected in these pages.

Someday Remember is just the beginning of Billy's journey; there are many adventures to come in this series. I am excited to share them with you all.

But most importantly, I want to express my heartfelt gratitude to my one true love, Bev Hall.

Meeting her was a turning point in my life, as she saw through the facade I presented and guided me with her unconditional love, patience, and understanding to where I stand today.

She is a remarkable woman who effortlessly inspires those around her and installs the belief that anything is possible if approached with the right mind-set.

Through her support and encouragement, I have overcome demons and thrived in ways I never thought possible.

Bev, my darling, I love you and I dedicate this book and all the hours of hard work poured into it to you. Thank you for being my rock and constant source of strength.

My hope is that everyone reading Someday Remember will take away a little piece of enjoyment from Billy's story.

Until next time...

www.ingramcontent.com/pod-product-compliance
Lightning Source LLC
Chambersburg PA
CBHW020650120726
47906CB00001B/212